The Christmas List

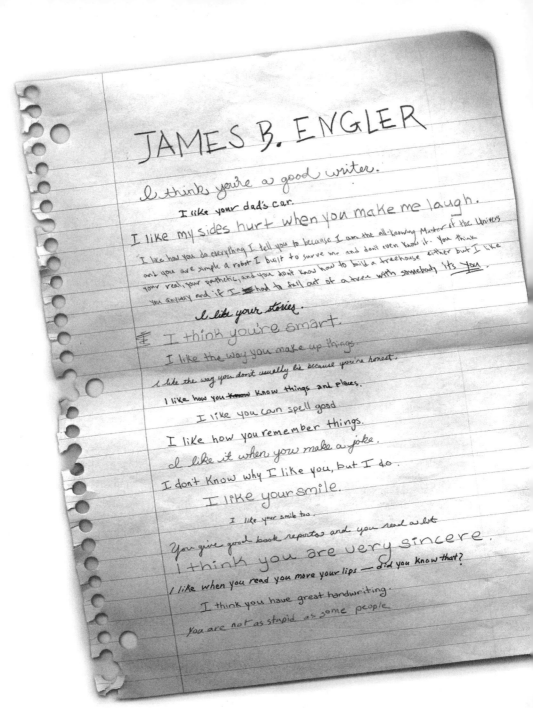

JAMES B. ENGLER

I think you're a good writer.

I like your dad's car.

I like my sides hurt when you make me laugh.

I like how you do everything I tell you to because I am the all-knowing Master of the Universe and you are simple a robot I built to surve me and don't even know it. You think you're real, your pathetic, and you don't know how to build a treehouse either but I like you anyway and if I ~~had~~ had to fall out of a tree with somebody ~~it's You~~.

I like your stories.

~~I~~ I think you're smart.

I like the way you make up things.

I like the way you don't usually lie because you're honest.

I like how you ~~know~~ know things and places.

I like you can spell good

I like how you remember things.

I like it when you make a joke.

I don't know why I like you, but I do.

I like your smile.

I like your smile too.

You give good book reports and you read a lot

I think you are very sincere.

I like when you read you more your lips — did you know that?

I think you have great handwriting.

You are not as stupid as some people

The Christmas List

PETE NELSON

RUTLEDGE HILL PRESS
Nashville, Tennessee
A Division of Thomas Nelson Publishers
Since 1798

www.thomasnelson.com

Published by Rutledge Hill Press, a Division of Thomas Nelson, Inc., P.O. Box 141000, Nashville, Tennessee 37214.

Scripture quotation in chapter 10 (Luke 2:1, 14) is from The New King James Version / Thomas Nelson Publishers, Nashville: Thomas Nelson Publishers, Copyright © 1982. Used by permission. All rights reserved.

Library of Congress Cataloging-in-Publication Data

Nelson, Peter, 1953–
  The Christmas list / Pete Nelson.
    p. cm.
  ISBN 1-4016-0143-X (hardcover)
  1. Funeral rites and ceremonies—Fiction. 2. Friendship—Fiction. I. Title.
  PS3614.E449C48 2004
  813'.54—dc22   2004004417

Printed in the United States of America
04 05 06 07 — 5 4 3 2 1

For Robert Wolk, teacher

Acknowledgments

I'D LIKE TO THANK AGENTS LANE ZACHARY AND TODD
Shuster of Zachary Shuster Harmsworth for their wise criticisms
and for their help in preparing the manuscript in the early drafts.
Thanks also go to Larry Stone, Jennifer Brett Greenstein, and
Anne Buchanan at Rutledge Hill Press for their efforts and assis-
tance in shepherding the manuscript through its various revi-
sions. I'd like to thank DeAnna Pierce and Bill Chiaravalle at
Brand Navigation for designing such an attractive cover. I'd also

like to thank and acknowledge the Franciscan Sisters of Little Falls (Minnesota) and particularly the late Sister Helen P. Mrosla, the fourth grade teacher in Morris, Minnesota, who originally gave the assignment to make a list and whose own account, "Thank You, Sister, for Teaching Me," continues to inspire and charm those who read it on the Internet and elsewhere. I'd like to thank my mother for sending me the newspaper clipping about Sister Mrosla that originally inspired me, and my sister Bekka for helping me with the Norwegian words. I am greatly and forever obliged to all the wonderful teachers I've had over the years who taught me and encouraged me to be a writer, including Mrs. Long in elementary school, Mr. Wolk in high school, Marilyn Nelson in college, and Richard Shelton, Hilma Wolitzer, Bharati Mukherjee, Janet Burroway, and others in graduate school. Finally, I need to thank my wife, Jennifer Gates, who has been both my best reader through the earliest drafts and my staunchest supporter through thick and thin, and my son, Jack, who sat in my lap and "helped" me type much of this.

The Christmas List

Prologue

BY THE TIME I GOT THE PHONE CALL, I WAS FAIRLY *stressed already. It was December 22, the last day of the semester. Classes had ended at noon, and now, in midafternoon, I was in my office, trying to wrap things up. I had grades to turn in and evaluations to complete, and I still had to inspect dorm rooms to make sure that nobody had left an illegal hot plate on or incense burning and that everything was shipshape for the break. I still had a few personal holiday details to attend to, last minute things to pick up or mail off. In addition, a bad storm had blown down from*

Canada, promising us as much as a foot of snow by midnight and threatening to shut down the airports, thereby altering the travel plans I'd made months ago and could not afford to change.

The call was from Patrick, a former student. He sounded desperate. I asked him what was wrong.

"Mr. Engler . . . would you mind if I came to talk to you?" he asked. "I think I really screwed up this time."

To be honest, my first thought was, Now? Are you kidding? I had, however, told him once that he should feel free to call me any time, day or night, if he ever needed to. I thought a moment. A moment was all it took to remember what's truly important, especially this time of year, and to put my other worries in perspective.

"Where are you calling from?" I asked.

"I'm in Manhattan, but I've got a car. I could be up there by five or six."

I teach at Mill River Academy, a boys' prep school in western Massachusetts, in the Berkshires. The town features a white clapboard church with black shutters and a white clapboard meeting hall, both facing the town common. There's also a brick post office with a Civil War–era cannon out front, positioned as if to attack the general store across the way. Inns and B&Bs and good restaurants ring the common, making the town a popular destination for autumn "leaf peepers." The school itself is all brick and ivy and sugar maples, with its own sugaring house for making Mill River Academy Grade A Golden Amber Syrup. Some of the faculty housing is more than two hundred years old. Outsiders think this is quaint. I've lived here for seventeen of the last twenty-seven years. It's starting to feel like home. I suspect it felt that way to Patrick too—as much a home as he ever knew.

Patrick was very bright and very funny in a wry and constructively sarcastic sort of way, a good writer who'd grown up in a dysfunctional family. His father was a high-achieving Washington lobbyist who traveled a great deal, his mother was some sort of D.C. socialite, and his two older sisters (whom I knew only through his stories) manifested a panoply of personality and affective disorders. Each year at semester's end, a transport van would arrive to take Patrick to the airport, where he'd be flown someplace for the holidays—a Caribbean island or a Colorado ski resort but never, to the best of my knowledge, home. His senior year, the staff found him lingering in his dorm after everyone else had gone. His father had forgotten to call the transport service. "I don't care," he told us. "He was probably too busy screaming at my mom. Or her lawyer. I think I'm just going to get a hotel room in New York."

It was, needless to say, a bluff. When I asked him if he wanted to stay with my wife and me instead, he readily agreed. Even before that, he'd occupied a special place in my heart. He was a gentle soul who sometimes thought too much, second-guessing himself and looking over his shoulder, sensitive to a fault. I had told him he could call me anytime, day or night, and reverse the charges if he had to—I suppose that included calling me two days before Christmas.

As Patrick spoke, I looked out my window at the quad. The snow was falling harder now, the lights in the buildings across from me a faint yellow in the blue blur of winter.

"I can't promise the roads are going to stay open," I said. "It looks pretty bad."

"I can make it," he said.

"Come on up, then," I said. "We'll be here."

I called my wife to give her a fair warning. "That was Patrick," I told her. "He's coming up. He needs to talk."

"I've got a pot of beef stew on the stove," she said. "Or is he still a vegetarian?"

"Last time I saw him, we had cheeseburgers," I told her.

WE HAD A FIRE GOING IN THE FIREPLACE WHEN THE doorbell sounded. Patrick's hair was wet. He wore neither hat, gloves, nor proper footwear.

"Are you all right?" I asked. "You look like you drove with the top down or something."

"*Actually,*" he said, stamping the snow off his shoes, "*I sort of went off the road about a mile back. The car's okay, but I had to walk. Can I use your phone?*"

While he called the garage, I located a bottle of sherry and gave him a glass to warm him. In the den, he propped his wet feet before the fire to dry. Sarah brought dinner in to us on trays, and Patrick ate like he hadn't had anything in days.

"*So what's going on?*" *I finally asked.* "*What gets you out in weather like this?*"

He looked at his food as he spoke.

"*Well,*" *he said,* "*to make a long story short, actually, I sort of dropped out of school again.*"

He looked at me for my reaction. The first time, he'd been a student at a big-name East Coast law school. He'd done his undergraduate degree in English at a school in California, three thousand miles away. California made him happy. Law school made his father happy. Patrick hated law school. He'd always loved to write, so we talked at the time about the idea of his transferring to the prestigious University of Iowa Writers' Workshop. Without telling his father, he applied and was accepted. I supported his decision. I agreed he couldn't live his life just to please his father. I told him, "*Do what you love and the money will follow*" *and* "*Do what you love and you'll never work a day in your life"*—nothing terribly original, but sound advice all the same. I think his mind had been made up about quitting law school before he even called me, but he was reassured when I seconded his decision.

"You're leaving Iowa, then," I gathered. "Can I ask why? Did something happen?"

"Actually, that's just it," he said. "Nothing happened. I can't write. I can't write anything. I don't belong there. I even turned in a piece I wrote as an undergraduate because I had to turn in something. I'm wasting everybody's time there. Including mine. It's embarrassing."

"Patrick," I said, "you know everybody feels that way when they're between things."

"What am I between?" he said. "I've done nothing in the past, and I'll do nothing in the future. I'm a complete fraud. I'm an impostor. With nothing to say."

"You have to realize that isn't true, even though you feel it is right now. Everybody—"

"—has something to say." He completed my sentence for me. "Well, I can't find it then. How am I supposed to go home? After I dropped out of law school, I thought my father was going to disown me or something. 'It's your life, Pat. You'd just better be damned sure you know what

you're doing with it,' he said. 'Oh, I am, Dad,' I said. 'Don't worry.'
Yeah, right."

"What does Ellen think?" asked Sarah, who had returned from the kitchen. She was referring to the art-student girlfriend Patrick had brought along when he visited the previous summer. He'd claimed they were just passing through town. My wife had known immediately that Patrick was thinking of Ellen in more permanent terms and that he'd brought her by to see what we thought of her. We liked her a lot.

"Ellen and I aren't talking," Patrick said. "We had a fight."

Sarah gave me a private look. We both knew there was something Patrick wasn't telling us.

"Was it a fight, or was it something more than that?" Sarah asked him.

"It was a little more than a fight. We were going to elope. We were supposed to meet at Grand Central and find a justice of the peace. But I panicked."

"And you left her waiting for you?" I asked. "In Grand Central Station?"

"I left a message on her voice mail," he said. "I couldn't reach her. Cell phones don't work in Grand Central."

Sarah closed her eyes and shook her head, then stood and picked up a tray to carry to the kitchen.

"I can't marry her," he said. "I'm just going to disappoint her. If not now, then sooner or later. I think I hurt her so badly that she'll never take me back. But that's good, because she should hate me. That way she'll move on faster and find somebody better."

"You told her that on her voice mail?" I asked. "Don't you think you should at least have told her that face-to-face?"

"Look, I know I screwed up. You don't have to tell me that. I just . . . I really don't know where to go. Or what to do."

"Well, until they tow your car out, I don't think you're going any-where," Sarah said. "Jim, why don't you tell him the story about the you-know-what."

Feeling a bit dense, I said I didn't know what.

"The list," she said.

"The Christmas list?"

She rolled her eyes.

"No, the grocery list," she said. "If you boys are all right, I'm going to go upstairs and wrap a few presents. Patrick, we'll put you on the hide-a-bed in the study."

When she had left the room, Patrick turned to me. "So what's this story?" he asked.

It was a good night for talking, so I told him. If the story touches on the *key to happiness or the "true meaning of Christmas" at any point, that is purely coincidental, because I can't say what either of those two things might be for anybody but myself. It is simply about another young man at Christmastime who felt he couldn't go home but then found that he could, in more ways than he'd ever thought possible.*

One

JAMES BENGT ENGLER, TWENTY-SEVEN, SAT IN HIS
car at a highway rest area about an hour from his home, watching snow fall and trying to compose his thoughts. It was Saturday
morning, December 23, 1990, and he'd been on the road almost
twenty-four hours. He'd stopped at a gas station in Youngstown,
Ohio, to call ahead and give his family a heads up, and again at
a Denny's in DeKalb, Illinois, but both times he had stopped in
mid-dial. He didn't know what to say to them.

Perhaps a little levity would help.

"Mom," he'd say, "Dad, good news! Catherine dumped me—more *lutefisk* for the rest of us."

No.

"Mom, Dad, I know you were expecting Catherine to be with me, but—"

But what?

Part of his problem was that each time he returned home, he felt on the spot anyway, as if more were expected of him than of his siblings—bringing up the rear of the family, as it were. And because he'd moved so far away, he felt he had to justify the move by achieving success.

Home was a town of 15,370 people, a farming community called Onagle, Iowa, just south of the Minnesota state line and an easy two-hour drive from Minneapolis/St. Paul. His family had been the richest family in town for almost one hundred years, owning Onagle Federal Savings, of which James's father, Walter Engler IV, was president. They lived in a brick, slate-roofed Queen Anne Victorian–style home near the country club. James was the youngest of five children, three boys and two girls, separated from his oldest sibling, Gerry (Walter Gerald) by a distance of sixteen years, though Gerry had died in 1972, when James was nine. Gerry had been a pilot, shot down over North Vietnam at the age of twenty-five.

The first Walter Engler, who was a great believer in learning and never thought much of the local schools, had begun the tradition of sending the boys in the family back east to be educated, to a place in western Massachusetts called Mill River Academy. As a result, some people in Onagle considered James's family to be standoffish or high-horsed or, at the very least, in violation of the concept of *jantaløven*, a Norwegian word meaning, approximately, "Don't-think-you're-better-than-anybody-else-but-don't-let-anybody-else-tell-you-they're-better-than-you." Some saw the Englers as standing apart from the community, despite the charity work James's mother and grandmother had always done, and despite a family history of philanthropy, and despite the family's active participation in the church, First Emmanuel Lutheran, where James's father was a deacon.

The irony was, at Mill River Academy, the Englers were considered ill-mannered, farm-boy hicks. Sometimes the ridicule was deserved. James Engler, for instance, had acquired the nickname "Otis" from his classmates when he'd gone down to New York

City with a group of school chums and tripped in a revolving door at Brooks Brothers. He'd been jammed in the door for a humiliating eight seconds, so his buddies had called him Otis, after Otis Elevators—as if elevators and revolving doors had anything in common.

Because they didn't fit in at school or in their hometown, the Engler men developed a kind of displaced loyalty to both, often extolling the simple virtues of small-town Midwestern life while at school but bragging about their East Coast adventures when they were back in Onagle, their outsider status partially self-imposed as a consequence. The massive home on the edge of town thus became a kind of family fortress. The house was the place they returned to, the spiritual center of everything, the sort of place that, had it been built in the South, would have been given its own name, like Tara or Ten Oaks or Longview. It stood on a hill surrounded by oak and black walnut trees, the property bounded by a road in front, woods to the north, fields to the east, and the country club to the south. Behind the house stood a barn and stables and, beyond the barn, a cottage for the hired handyman, a lean and deliberate fellow in his late sixties named Cully (Culligan, first name Bert). Cully had worked for the railroad in his youth. Now he farmed two hundred acres leased from a neighbor in addition to helping out at the Engler place.

The main house had seven bedrooms, six baths, five fireplaces, four balconies, three porches, two garages, and one hard and fast rule: Everybody had to come home for Christmas. No exceptions and no excuses allowed short of hospitalization in an ICU—with at least one limb at risk for amputation.

THAT WAS WHY JAMES, ON DECEMBER 23, 1990, WAS sitting in his car at the highway rest area wondering what to say to his family. Technically, he wouldn't be breaking the rule by arriving without his fiancée, the woman he'd introduced to the family the year before. She was not yet a member of the family in the legal sense. Yet they'd welcomed her as such, telling her how glad they were that little Jimmy had finally found his soul mate, joking how they'd begun to worry if he'd ever meet the right person. He wished he hadn't used the term *soul mate* when he'd first spoken of her. At any rate, they would expect to see her. His family would want an explanation. And how could he tell them the truth?

"Mom, Dad, I wanted to tell you before—the engagement is off. She didn't believe in me any more. And neither did I."

Something like that.

He felt, more than ever, like a failure, the black sheep, the problem child, the lone loser in a long line of successful marriages and relationships. No one in his family had ever been divorced. No one had called off an engagement or been dumped on the way to the altar. No one had truly blown it . . . until now.

He couldn't sit by the side of the road forever. Finally he turned the key in the ignition and steered carefully back onto the highway, still not knowing what to say but hoping he'd think of something when the time came.

He turned into the long driveway around noon, wondering who'd be there to greet him. His oldest sister, Lisa, and her husband, Joe, and their two children, Kirstin and Abigail (eight and six), had arrived the day before from Minneapolis, where Joe was the manager of a large suburban branch of Twin City Federal. Lisa was blonde, blue-eyed, and, for the first fourteen years of his life, James's least favorite sibling baby-sitter, a strict enforcer of bedtimes and parental TV-viewing injunctions. The only kid in the family who'd been a member of 4-H, she was a champion gardener now, specializing in roses. Where Lisa was relentlessly serious and would at best arch an eyebrow upon hearing the world's funniest joke, Joe was one of the world's most cheerful individuals, always singing or whistling to himself.

James's older (and balder) brother, Eric—a Republican and a bank vice president, and a three-handicap golfer despite the fact that he never fudged the rules or took mulligans—was due in from Denver that afternoon. He and his wife, Rachel, and their three boys, Paul, Thomas, and Henry (ten, nine, and five) would arrive in Minneapolis around four and then drive down in a rented car.

At his best, James was happy for his siblings' successes, their families, and all the substantial things they'd done with their lives. At his worst, he was envious and felt like a failure in comparison. His sister Julie, of course, was still single, but even Julie was a force to be reckoned with. Two years older than him and an artist, she was driving in from Chicago and due to arrive some time that afternoon, depending on the roads. Eight inches of snow had already fallen, and it was still coming down. Julie drove a red canvas-top Jeep with fat, knobby tires, and she'd told everybody that nothing would stop her. Considering how she liked to load her Jeep with camping gear and blank canvases and drive off by herself to remote wilderness locations to paint landscapes for weeks at a time, James had no doubt she'd make it through a mere eight inches of snow.

The long, tree-lined driveway made James feel at home, but it also made him feel, as he reached the end of it, disappointed in himself as he looked up at the grand house and compared it to the tiny Greenwich Village apartment he could barely afford, even with Catherine splitting the rent with him. He'd known at an early age that he would never be as financially astute as his father or brother. He'd never developed an interest in the family business of banking. Growing up, he'd felt his eyes glaze over when dinner-table talk turned to interest rates or the stock market, and even now he was effectively innumerate, unable to so much as balance his checkbook. For as long as he could remember he'd wanted to be a writer, and his parents, to their credit, had always encouraged his literary propensities—or rather, his mother had encouraged them. His father had told his friends at the country club, "Jimmy's long-term plan is to become a college professor one day." This, at the time, had been entirely Walter Engler's invention.

The problem was, James had been having serious doubts of late that he could make even a meager living as either a writer or as a teacher. His teaching assistantship stipend barely covered his half of the basic necessities. Catherine worked as a para-legal, but even with two incomes, they never had enough money. He'd sold a short story to the *New Yorker* around the time he'd first met Catherine, but since then he'd produced very little and was starting to question his abilities. Their financial worries had caused tension between them—or maybe the fights over money were just a small part of something larger. The previous month had been pure hell, full of long arguments, raised voices, sad conversations, refusals, denials, somber realizations, blame casting and finger pointing, lost sleep, lost appetites, ignored phone messages, and neglected duties. The six months before that hadn't been so great either. He'd climbed into his car for the long drive home for Christmas knowing that, sometime in his absence, Catherine would remove her things from their apartment, slip her key under the door, and move into her own apartment.

Perhaps he'd think of some way to win her back. Perhaps she'd change her mind on her own. Maybe they needed to shake things up a little. Or maybe what they had was broken and couldn't be fixed.

"You and Catherine can sleep in your room," his mother

had told his answering machine a few weeks prior to his leaving. "Your father and I talked about it, and I know we've always said we wanted our kids to be married before they slept together under our roof, but since you two are practically married already and living together, we thought it would be all right."

She'd added, "Also, if you don't mind, we'd like to have some friends over for an informal little engagement party for you two—nothing fancy—sometime before New Year's, so let me know if there's anyone you want us to invite. Looking forward to seeing you."

He'd gone incommunicado after that, but he knew he should have said something.

He parked behind Joe and Lisa's Caravan, shut off the engine, grabbed his coat from the seat beside him, and went to face everybody. He remembered how excited he'd been, getting out of the car the year before with Catherine at his side.

So much could change in a year.

Two

LISA AND JOE'S GIRLS, KIRSTIN AND ABIGAIL, WERE
sledding in the front yard. They had white-blonde hair and upturned
noses and wore bright, wide smiles and matching fuzzy white ear-
muffs that belonged in an Elvis Presley movie. They ran to him
and gave him big hugs.

"I got ice skates," Abigail said. "Maybe we could go?"

"Maybe we could," James said. "I think I still have a pair down in
the basement. We'll have to wait for them to plow the rink, though."

"Where's Aunt Catherine?" they wanted to know.

"Catherine won't be coming this year," James replied.

"Where is she?"

"She's going to be spending Christmas with her family," James told his nieces, smiling. "Where's your mom?"

They pointed to the house. He shouldered his bag and walked, trying to keep his head up, telling himself it was good to be home, come what may. He'd kept his family in the dark, hoping up to the last minute that things would work out and they'd never have to know what a mess he'd made of things.

Lisa and Ruth, James's mother, were in the kitchen having cocoa. Lisa, always colder than anybody else in the room, huddled in a heavy sweater while she sipped from her mug, which she cupped in both hands for warmth. His mother studied a cookbook recipe, her narrow reading glasses perched on the end of her nose in a way that always made her look like Mrs. Santa Claus. (When not in use, they hung by a thin chain around her neck.) She had to tip her head forward and peer over the top of her glasses to see him.

"Jimmy," she said. "Oh, it's so good to see you! Your hair's gotten darker."

She said this every time she saw him, even though his hair hadn't changed its hue since he was seven or eight. She hugged him as he dropped his bag on the floor. Then she looked for his fiancée, glancing out the window to see if Catherine might be unloading the car.

"Catherine won't be joining us," he announced.

"She won't?" his mother said, eyes wide, not yet getting it. She wore a worried expression. "Where is she?"

"Well, I think they're in Manhattan, but there was talk of going somewhere," James said. "I'll fill you in later. Everything's all right. Okay if I put my stuff in my old room?"

He wasn't sure why he said, "Everything's all right," when clearly everything wasn't.

His mother was too confused to say anything. Lisa looked surprised.

"Hey, baby brother," she said, "come here." She hugged him with one arm, holding her cocoa out so as not to spill it. "We're glad you could make it." She looked him in the eye and by her expression—raised eyebrows and a single blink, head tilted back and slightly to the side—managed to say, "You and I both know there's more we should talk about, but not in front of Mom, if you'd prefer."

"Hey, Jimbo," his brother-in-law, Joe, called out from the mudroom. "Drive okay? You must be beat." He was donning a red-and-black plaid wool coat that hung loosely on his trim frame. "Feel up to helping your dad and Cully and me cut down a tree?"

"We're not waiting for Eric?"

"Be dark by the time he gets here," Joe said. "We were planning a little tree-trimming party for tonight." James noticed a bowl of popped popcorn and bags of cranberries waiting to be strung.

"Let me put my stuff away, and I'll get my boots." he said, glad for the diversion.

"Don't let your father do any heavy lifting," his mother warned. "I worry enough about him with that ax. Are you sure you're all right?"

"A little exercise will be good for me," James told her, knowing that wasn't what she meant.

His room upstairs was as clean as a hospital room. He had known it would be. His mother kept his room just as it had been when he'd last occupied it, as she did for all her children. James dropped his bags on his bed, crossed the hall, and opened the door to Gerry's room, where Eric's boys would be sleeping.

The model airplanes that once hung suspended from the ceiling on fishing line, perhaps as many as fifty, were gone, and the holes in the plaster overhead had been spackled over and the ceiling repainted, but the rest was the same. On the wall behind the bed were the autographed pictures of Minnesota sports legends Fran Tarkington and Harmon Killebrew, along with Gerry's framed acceptance letter to the Air Force Academy and a mounted photograph of Gerry in uniform. His medals and his various football and baseball trophies sat on the shelves, and with them a Wilson baseball mitt—Roberto Clemente model—that looked brand new. The mitt had been among Gerry's effects when the Air Force had shipped them home.

James made a habit of looking into Gerry's room when he was home, just to help him remember. His eye lingered only a moment longer, this time on a framed black-and-white photograph of Gerry, Eric, Lisa, Julie, and James in their snowsuits, sledding one Christmas morning long ago at a place on the golf course's fourteenth fairway they'd called Dead Man's Hill. They called it that because it was long and steep and had a creek at the bottom, protected by a hump that could get a toboggan airborne if you hit it wrong—or right, if airborne was what you wanted. Gerry had always led the sledding parties, which was why no one had gone since he'd died. No one called it Dead Man's Hill anymore, either. James wondered if the hill was where his brother first fell in love with flying.

HE CAUGHT UP TO THE LOGGING CREW IN THE BARN, where his father was using an electric grinding wheel to sharpen a double-bladed ax that had been in the family for as long as anybody could remember. Cully was there, wearing the same janitor-green shirt and pants he'd always worn, with a greasy, quilted down jacket on over it and a matching cap on his head, cocked jauntily to one side. Joe stood in the doorway, whistling "Venite Adoremus" as he waited.

Cully smiled warmly when he saw James. "Well, look what the storm blowed in," he said. Cully was a self-educated man with shelves of classical texts and history books he'd picked up in used bookstores over the years. He'd even taught James how to play chess as a boy. Yet when he spoke, he resorted to slang and colloquialisms, more as a matter of regional pride than anything else. "How them crazy New Yorkers treating you?"

"Pretty good," James replied, thinking, *All but one.* "I can't complain. Merry Christmas."

Cully nodded back.

James's father kept to his work, unable to hear anything over the sound of the grinder. James thought his father's hair looked whiter. He watched the sparks fly where stone ground against steel and he thought, as he'd thought since he was young, that the sparks must hurt his father's bare hands. They never did—or if they did, his father never said so. The official tree could only be hewn with the official ax, even though his father owned two chainsaws. Finally, his father shut the grinder off, satisfied that the edge of the ax was sharp enough. The wheel spun down, making the bench it was fastened to rumble.

"Hey, Pops," James said, "need some help?"

"Hello, James," his father said. Walter Engler was not one for hugging. He set the ax down to don a pair of sheepskin mittens. "How was the drive?"

"Good," James said. "Ohio lasts forever, but other than that."

"Catherine won't be joining us?" his father asked as he emerged from the barn with the ax over his shoulder, clad in high-laced, black, army-issue snow boots, gray wool pants tucked into the boots, a green parka, and a purple wool Minnesota Vikings stocking cap pulled down low over his bushy eyebrows. The gold wire-rimmed glasses over his intense charcoal-gray eyes made him look vaguely military, and James noticed that his jawline was still relatively free of the wattles men his age often sported, though his nose was turning to strawberry from broken capillaries.

"She's in New York, with her family," James said, volunteering no more than the basic facts.

"I see," his father replied, and then he walked off into the snow, head down to the wind, Cully right behind him. Walter Engler, like many Scandinavian men, lacked both aptitude and experience when it came to discussing feelings, his own or anybody else's. A large man, he had been a tackle on his college football team. He still stood an unstooped six-foot-four and was fit for sixty-six years of age, though he seldom exercised, and trim, though he didn't watch his diet.

"Two things. . . ." Joe's voice came from behind. James waited for him to catch up. They followed James's father and Cully toward the woods but lagged until they were out of earshot. When they were out of view from the house, Joe reached into his pocket, pulled out a pack of cigarettes, and lit one. Lisa knew he smoked, and he was trying to quit, but until he could, he'd agreed to smoke only outdoors and in places where the girls couldn't see him.

"Yeah?"

"Don't mention the Larsons' party," Joe said quietly.

"Why not?" James asked. The Larsons were the second richest family in town, owners of the John Deere tractor and farm implement dealership, the Agway, and the grain elevator. Their son, Ben, had been a classmate of James's. Their annual Christmas party was, by some accounts, the social occasion of the year.

"Because they're not going."

"When is it?"

"Tonight."

"So why aren't they going?"

"Because they weren't invited."

"How could they not be invited?"

Joe shrugged. "Lisa told your folks it was probably an oversight and they should go anyway, but your mother says you don't go unless you get an official invitation, even if you think it was an oversight."

Walking through the snow left James panting, his breath sending clouds of steam into the woods with each step he took. Joe, also out of shape, breathed heavily through his nose.

"How could they not be invited?" James asked again. "They've known the Larsons their whole lives. Who's going to sing with the Merry Madrigals?" He referred to a barbershop quartet comprising his father, Gene Larson, Pastor Gruening from church, and Tom Brown, a local farmer.

"I don't know. Lisa said she heard Tom Brown hasn't been feeling so good, so he probably isn't going to make it anyway."

"Did they have a falling out?"

"Not with the Larsons." Joe took one last drag from his cigarette, pinched the ember off with his fingers, and stashed the butt in an empty mint tin he produced from his back pocket. "Cully thinks it's the economy, if you know what I mean."

James indeed knew what Joe meant. In the eighties, his family's bank had made a lot of loans to farmers who'd used their farms as collateral. That was back when interest rates were artificially low, when corn and bean prices reached record highs, and when farmland, for a number of reasons, had reached an inflated value of up to two thousand dollars an acre, creating a county of "paper millionaires." When interest rates rose again and the price of farmland and corn and beans dropped back to more realistic levels, borrowers had found themselves without the equity they'd borrowed against or the income they needed to make their payments. The bank, obligated to protect its investors and shareholders, found itself forced to call in its unsecured loans or risk becoming undercapitalized. Some people who didn't understand the complexities of the matter would drive by the Engler house, see it standing on the hill like some unassailable castle, and think the Engler family was looking out for number one and didn't give a damn about the community.

The local economy was still shaking down—folks struggling, declaring bankruptcy, selling to larger incorporated farms, taking losses, despairing. To make matters worse, the previous summer had, like the summer before, brought an extended drought that had reduced yields by as much as 50 percent in some areas. At a time of year when you could see the lights on in the farmhouse kitchens late at night, everybody doing their books and trying to figure out next year's budget, the bank still had to be paid first, and some families had been forced to cancel vacation plans, drop their health insurance, or cut back on things like Christmas presents. The Larsons might well have been told, in so many words, that some of their guests would not feel entirely comfortable attending the party if Walter and Ruth Engler were invited.

"That stinks," James said. "What's the second thing?"

"Your friend Sarah called."

Sarah was Tom Brown's daughter, one of two hometown friends James had managed to stay in touch with over the years.

"When?"

"This morning. She said she knew you'd be coming home, and she wanted you to call her."

"She's here in Onagle?"

"Apparently."

"Did she say what it was about?"

"Something about your friend Mike," Joe said. "She said you'd know what it was about." The other friend James had stayed in touch with was Mike Quinn. James had been looking forward to Mike's annual post-Christmas white-elephant swap.

"Probably about the party," James said. "She left me a message in New York, but I never called her back. This is good. Last year the air force didn't let him come home, and we didn't have it."

"You and this Sarah person been in touch?" Joe asked, waggling his eyebrows. "She wouldn't be an old flame, would she?"

"Sarah?" James laughed.

"What's so funny?"

"Combination of things," James said. He laughed in part because he felt a million miles away from thinking of anyone that way, let alone Sarah Brown. "I've known Sarah since kindergarten," he told Joe. "She was always a total tomboy. The word *flame* doesn't apply. Though she did chase me one time for pushing her marshmallow into the fire when we were making s'mores."

Thinking back, he recalled that Sarah had chased him a lot when they were kids—not because she was sweet on him, but because she loved to run. She was the only girl who could beat him in a foot race on the playground or climb higher in a tree than he could. When he once teased her by saying she had a crush on him, she had blushed beet red and denied it vehemently. Throughout their childhood, she'd remained a friend. She'd been the one who predicted the tree house he and Mike had built, held together with ropes instead of nails to spare the tree, wouldn't hold, but who refrained from saying "I told you so" when they fell out of it because James broke his clavicle in the fall and it hurt him to laugh. He was glad to hear she was in town. Last he knew, she was living in Hawaii.

"You and Sarah never dated, then?" Joe asked.

"Nope," James said. Up ahead, his father paused, gazing through the trees, looking for the right one to cut down. "If we'd dated, we'd probably have broken up and never talked to each other again."

In fact, the issue of dating had never really come up. By the time interest in the opposite sex began to dawn on them, James had gone east for school and Sarah had stayed behind. They became pen pals and wrote each other about the various people they were romantically inclined toward. In high school, against James's advice, Sarah dated Ben Larson. Ben was a bit of a grade-school bully but oddly inconsistent about it, nice and funny most of the time but sporadically nasty, the kind of kid who'd pay you three or four compliments and then insult you or say something that hurt. Ben had always been jealous those summers when James came home to resume his friendship with Sarah, which was platonic but still more conversationally intimate than anything Ben was getting.

The summer before college, in particular, they had spent a lot of time together, and perhaps there was a small spark or an appreciation of what they had and stood a chance of losing, but in the end they knew they were about to go their separate ways— James to Brown and Sarah to UCLA—and they wanted to keep things simple. The first week of August, they carried a six-pack up to the top of Sarah's father's drying bin, where they sipped beers, gazed across the rippling fields, and watched the sun set so red it looked like the whole sky had caught fire. When Sarah confessed her fear that she'd never see him again, he reminded her they'd always see each other at Christmas.

It hadn't happened that way. After college, Sarah had moved to Hawaii, and she didn't make it home that much any more.

"Well, she called," Joe said. "She said it was important."

WALTER AND CULLY WERE EXAMINING A TALL BLUE spruce when James and Joe caught up with them. They circled the tree, examining it from every angle.

"That's a nice one, Walter," said Cully, who was never much of a talker.

"It looks pretty symmetrical," Joe said. "Good and full too."

"A little nasty at the top," James said, "but we can always give it a haircut once we get it down."

James and Joe held back the lower branches as best they could while James's father swung the ax. Joe whistled "O Christmas Tree" as the chips flew. When the tree fell, the younger men dragged it, fat end first, back to the house, retracing their footprints in the snow. James's father followed, the ax over his shoulder.

In the barn, James helped Cully cut the tree to its proper nine-foot-six-inch length, lopping the lower branches off with the smaller chainsaw.

"We could have cut the tree down in half the time if we'd used the chainsaw in the first place," James said.

"You in a hurry?" Cully asked him. "Besides, that wouldn't have been tradition."

"I've got nothing against tradition, as long as it makes sense," James said.

Cully handed him a can of turpentine to wash the pine pitch from his hands. James dried his hands on a paper towel.

"Sometimes you do stuff just 'cause it's stuff you always do," Cully said.

"That's something I've never understood," James said.

Cully looked at him and smiled, patting him on the arm.

"You will," he said.

Three

JAMES HELPED MOUNT THE TREE IN ITS STAND,
then retired to his room. All at once a feeling of exhaustion came
over him. He'd slept very little the night before, in a Super 8
motel in Illinois with spiders in the shower and a TV remote that
didn't work. He'd lain awake, feeling sorry for himself, thinking
of all the reasons why Catherine thought their relationship
wasn't working—that they didn't share the same interests or
schedules, that they didn't really talk anymore, that they just

couldn't seem to get along, despite their recent attempt at seeing a counselor. They'd come to live parallel lives, with Catherine working overtime while James ate dinner in front of the television alone or James grading papers while Catherine worked out at the gym or Catherine joining her friends on Fire Island for a weekend while James stayed home at the computer. That sort of thing, until they were never together anymore, despairing in their worst moments and quietly fraternal in their best. She told him she felt like he kept pushing her away, keeping her at a distance.

He knew that men of Scandinavian descent had a perhaps deserved reputation for being emotionally remote, though the women who grew up around them seemed to be able to see through that. Compared to my father, he wanted to argue, I'm a veritable fountain of emotion and sentimentality. Her charge that he was defensive was aggravating, a Catch-22 kind of accusation where to deny the charge, by definition, proved it. He'd tried to employ a live-and-let-live philosophy, which Catherine took to mean he didn't care or wasn't involved. The conclusion he reached was that maybe he just didn't know how to live in a relationship. Yet it wasn't something he could go off somewhere and learn by himself.

Sitting down on his old bed, he took off his boots, then leaned back on the bedspread to close his eyes just for a second. A horn honking in the driveway woke him up. He looked out the window and saw a red Jeep, then quickly slipped his feet into a pair of old moccasins and went downstairs.

Julie was physically the opposite of Lisa, shorter and rounder, and with black hair instead of Lisa's blonde. Her choice of lipstick was a darker burgundy color, and she favored hoop earrings and silver chains, while Lisa wore diamond studs and raw pearls.

He met her in the front hall.

"Hey Jules," he said as she doffed her stocking cap and shook her hair free, "I almost called you on my way through town last night, but it was after midnight." He had an open invitation to stay at her house, but he was also allergic to cats, and she had four. In the warmer months, he could crash on her front porch, but he was physically incapable of spending more than ten minutes inside her apartment.

"I was still up," she said, "wrapping, wrapping." She pointed to the two overstuffed green garbage bags in the hallway. He grabbed one.

"Wait, wait," she said. "One's presents and one's laundry. Here, take this one. And this one goes into the basement."

He helped her drag the bag of presents into the den, where the tree had been installed in its corner, though no presents could be put under it until it had been fully trimmed. Boxes of lights and ornaments waited on the coffee table.

The garbage bag's drawstrings loosened as they tucked it into a corner. James took a small package from the bag and examined it. Julie was the most inventive present wrapper in the family, always tying candies or small plastic animals in with the multi-colored ribbons. This year, she'd drawn elaborate pen-and-ink cartoons on all the packages, coloring them in with watercolors and using some sort of heavy stock art paper. It must have taken her hours to do each present.

"Are we supposed to open these or frame the wrapping paper?" he asked.

"It's conceptual art," she answered facetiously, reaching to hug him now that her hands were free. "Actually, there's nothing inside."

"Really?" he said, feeling immediately gullible.

"No, not really," she said. "Wow. You've gained weight."

"So kind of you to notice. You look dramatically older."

"It probably only seems like you've gained weight because your head's gotten pointier."

"You probably only look older because your butt's started to sag, but I do like the zit on the end of your nose. Is that some sort of Rudolph thing you've done for the holidays?"

"Okay, you win," she said. She hugged him again.

They'd greeted each other in approximately this way since middle school.

Ruth Engler interrupted to give her youngest daughter a welcoming kiss, then started picking cat hairs and pieces of lint from her coat. Julie met James's eyes and grinned. Their mother's habit of constantly tidying up was an old source of amusement.

"I just called the airline," their mother said. "Eric and Rachel's flight is still on time. I'm surprised. I was afraid they were going to close the airport."

"Where's Cath?" Julie whispered.

"Tell you later," James whispered back.

"You wanna drive up to meet 'em?" Julie asked.

"I thought they were renting a car," he said.

"Yeah, but let's meet 'em at the gate." She gave him a meaningful look, by which James understood that she wanted to talk. He didn't know how to refuse.

As soon as they were in her Jeep, she reached across, put her hand on the back of his neck, and gave him an affectionate squeeze. She asked what was going on.

"I mean, I haven't seen Catherine in a year, but I really thought you guys looked . . . happy."

"We were," he said.

"Really?"

He thought a moment.

"Off and on we were," James said. He thought harder. "Actually, I remember thinking you're supposed to feel good when you're engaged to somebody, but all I felt was nervous. I was always thinking about everything that could go wrong."

"So what did?"

"Where do you want me to start? She thinks I don't like her friends," James said. "For one thing."

He stared out the window as he spoke, watching the snow sweep across the fields from the west and drift up against the fence line on the right side of the road, a white landscape beneath a white sky, farmhouses shielded behind their wind-breaks. The Jeep held the road, the heater blasting on high.

"Do you?" his sister asked.

"I like them fine, and they like me, or at least I thought they did."

"Then why'd she say that?"

"'Cause I was jealous of them, I suppose," he admitted. "Because she could talk to them and not to me."

"If she couldn't talk to you, that's her fault too," she said. "That's why they call it '*co*-mmunication.' They don't call it 'munication.'"

"That's not even a word."

"You know what I mean. It's a two-way street. You both send and you both receive. It's a system that requires two people."

"Whatever it is, it broke down," he said. And it's not Catherine's fault. It's me. I didn't pay enough attention. I didn't make her feel special."

"Oh, spare me," Julie said. "And while you're at it, go a little easier on yourself. If one person in a relationship, out of the blue, has an affair or starts robbing convenience stores or something, then yeah, maybe you can talk about whose fault it is. But if two intelligent people who care about each other try really hard and it still doesn't work out, don't talk about who's to blame for this or that, because it's useless. If you ask me, it's fifty-fifty. You didn't rob any convenience stores, did you?"

"Just one," he said. "It was a little one."

"What did Mom say?"

"About robbing the convenience store? She was against it."

"You know what I mean."

"She was surprised. Given that she only found out today."

"You didn't tell anybody she called off the engagement?"

"I was going to."

"You could have at least told me, you know. Or any of us."

"I was waiting to see."

"What'd Dad say?"

"Very little. Not that I was expecting more."

"And Mom didn't say anything?"

"I've mostly managed to avoid her so far."

"You can talk to Mom about this sort of thing, you know," Julie said. "At least I always could. She's pretty sharp about relationships, believe it or not."

"By the way," James said. "Don't mention the Larsons to

Mom or Dad. The party is tonight, but they weren't invited this year."

THE TWIN CITIES AIRPORT WAS UNDER CONSTRUCTION, so parking took a while, but they still managed to meet Eric and his family at the gate on the red concourse. Thomas and Henry ran to give their Uncle James and Aunt Julie each a hug. Paul hung back, old enough now to feel embarrassed by public displays of affection. James offered him a hand to shake. The boys were dark like their mother, the opposite of their fair-haired cousins.

"I don't believe you guys drove all the way up here in the snow!" Rachel exclaimed, but James could tell they were all pleased at the welcome committee. "Did Catherine remember to bring a good pair of winter boots this time?" Rachel asked as they all headed toward the baggage area. Rachel and Catherine had hit it off the year before and had looked forward to becoming sisters-in-law. Rachel, who was Jewish and from a large city, Denver, had even promised to teach Catherine how to feel like less of an outsider in the rural Midwest. Wearing fully functional footwear was a start.

"Catherine's not coming," James said.

"Oh, no," his sister-in-law said. "She couldn't make it? Is everything okay?"

"No, she's fine," James said. "We're going through a rocky spell." Why couldn't he just come out and say it was over?

"We went over the Rockies in a plane," Henry said.

"No, we didn't, Henry," Rachel said. "From where we live, we'd have to fly west to fly over the Rockies. We were flying east."

"East!" Henry said gleefully, and then he chased his brother Tom around the baggage carousel.

Eric put his arm around his brother's shoulder and hugged him.

"Sucky time of year to go through something like that," Eric said.

"Next June would have been *so* much better," James agreed. "Maybe opening day of baseball season—that'd be a good day to be dumped."

"So what happened?"

"If you don't mind, I'd rather not talk about it. Julie and I talked about it on the way up, and I'm burnt out."

"Okay," Eric said. "Actually, I have to say I'm a little bit relieved."

"Why?"

"Because now everybody won't be talking about me."

He faced his siblings and, with a flourish, removed his Irish tweed walking cap, which came down well over his ears and collar, to reveal that he was now wearing a toupee.

"You shaved your mustache," James deadpanned.

"Oh, come on, gimme your best shot," Eric said. "Let's get it over with. Make a joke. Ask me if I know I have a dead squirrel on my head."

"No, really," James said, "it looks very good. You look twenty years younger. I'm serious."

"You know you want to make a joke, so just make it," Eric insisted.

"I don't," James said. "I like it."

"Daddy says we're not supposed to touch his hair unless it's in the box," Henry shouted loudly enough for everyone waiting at the baggage carousel to hear.

Eric tried not to, but soon blushed a bright and Christmassy red. James and Julie tried not to laugh but couldn't stop themselves, their giggles bursting uncontrollably into guffaws. Even Rachel had to hide her face, shushing Henry, though it was too late. Eric's face continued to burn as James and Julie struggled to stop laughing.

James didn't really want to stop because it was the first time he'd truly laughed in what had to be weeks. His sorrows would return soon enough, he suspected.

four

AFTER DINNER, IT WAS TIME TO TRIM THE TREE.
Each spouse, child, and grandchild had a designated ornament
that only he or she could hang. Catherine had been assigned an
ornament as well. James saw Julie quietly slip it back into the
box. He gave her a look and a weak smile to say, *Thanks for doing
that.* Once the lights were strung and the ornaments were on the
tree, Walter would climb the stepladder to mount the glass angel
at the top of the tree, and then the task would be completed.

"I'm so sorry all this is happening to you now," his mother said to James when they found themselves alone for a moment. She squeezed his hand. "Christmas is supposed to be a time of joy. Well, at least you're home."

"I'm glad to be home," he told her, not realizing yet what she meant by "all this." He assumed she was only referring to his problems with Catherine. He only realized what his mother was talking about, and why his family had been so solicitous, when he spoke to his friend Sarah. He used the phone in his father's den. He didn't have to look the number up because he'd known it since he was six.

"Hey, J.B.," she said.

"Hey," he said. "What's new? How's Hawaii?"

"Don't know," she said. "I live here now. I moved home to help my mom when my dad broke his hip. . . ."

"Here?" he said. "In Onagle? Wow. I had no idea. When did you move?"

There was a long pause. "Listen, J.B., I've been trying to call you."

"Yeah, Joe said you called."

"No, I called you in New York. You didn't get the message? I left it on your machine."

"I got it," he admitted. "I'm really sorry I didn't get back to you. Nothing personal. I haven't been calling anybody back because there's been a lot going on. I'll tell you all about it. I figured I'd call you when I got to town." Even as he said it, he realized Sarah was exactly the person he could talk to about Catherine. "You wanna go get a beer or something?"

"Oh, my God," she said. "You don't know, do you? You haven't heard."

"Heard what?"

"About Mike. Your folks didn't say anything?"

"I had a message to call my mom, but I didn't call her back either. Why? What about Mike? What's wrong? Something's wrong."

"About as wrong as it gets," she said. "That's why I couldn't leave it on your machine. Mike died, J.B. I'm really sorry."

"What?" he said. He was stunned. "How? What? Start over. When?"

"His helicopter crashed," Sarah said. "They flew the body home last week."

For a long time, he couldn't say anything.

"From where?"

"He'd been over in the Persian Gulf. He was on a training mission. I'm still not clear if it was a sandstorm or if the helicopter he was in had some sort of mechanical failure. The paper seemed to say it was both."

James had wondered to what extent Mike was going to be involved in the conflict looming in the Middle East, and he'd worried about him. A coalition of armed forces had been gathering in the area for months now, preparing to oust the occupying Iraqi troops from Kuwait. The newspapers, Sarah said, were calling the victims of the crash—Mike, three of his crewmembers, and a British observer—the first casualties of the conflict. James hadn't been paying much attention to the newspapers of late either.

"You still there?" Sarah asked him.

"Yeah," he said. "I was going to say, 'You're kidding,' but of course you're not. It's just . . . unbelievable."

"I couldn't agree more."

"How're Mike's parents holding up? Is there anything I could do? Anything they need?"

"I took a hot dish over to the house, but it seemed like they had plenty of friends helping out. From the look of things, they're hanging in there. His sisters are all home."

"When's the funeral?"

"Tuesday," she said. "They're calling it a memorial service. At St. Mary's. And then an even more informal thing at the Supper Club. Mike said he didn't want a funeral, so I guess it's sort of a compromise. We all know he wouldn't have minded a party."

"You're right about that."

"The news hit pretty hard. It's like everybody knew him. They even sent a TV crew down from Minneapolis. People wanted to do something, so we figured we'd have one last white-elephant bash in his honor. I guess *bash* isn't the right word, and I don't think we'll do the white-elephant thing. . . ."

"Listen, Sarah," he said, "we should get together. Can you meet me at the Supper Club in an hour or so?"

"Sure," she said. "I think things are under control here."

When his mother came up the stairs bearing a brace of shopping bags full of empty ornament boxes, he followed her up into the cold attic where he'd played any number of games as a child. He remembered playing *Man from U.N.C.L.E.* in the attic with Mike Quinn, the two of them flipping the caps of their pens and saying "Open channel D" into their pretend communicators.

"I feel like such a jerk," he told his mother. "I just got off the phone with Sarah. I didn't know about Mike. I just found out now."

"Oh, dear," his mother said, looking at him with surprise. She set the empty boxes down and hugged him. "You didn't get my letter? I sent you the newspaper clipping."

"I got it," he apologized. "It's sitting on my kitchen table along with all the rest of my unopened mail. I thought it was your annual newsletter, so I figured I'd read it when I got here."

"Well, I'm just sorry you had to find out this way."

"It's nobody's fault but mine," he said.

HE WENT DOWNSTAIRS. HE PASSED HIS FATHER ON THE second floor landing and thought the old man looked troubled somehow, with a kind of lost expression. When James smiled, his father nodded but said nothing, then made his way down the hall and closed his bedroom door behind him.

In the kitchen, James saw a neatly stacked plate of sugar cookies that Abigail and Kirstin had helped their grandmother make and decorate. The girls, in oversized aprons, were washing the dishes.

"Come on, girls," their mother said, entering the kitchen. "Time for bed. Look at your cousin Henry—he's already in his P.J.s." Henry was helping his cousins by eating the broken cookies.

"But Grandma told us we had to help clean up," Kirstin told her.

"I'll help Grandma this time," Lisa told them. "You two need to get to bed."

"You hear about Mike Quinn?" James asked his sister.

"Uh-huh," Lisa said, grimacing sympathetically but obviously reluctant to talk about it in front of the children. "I ran into his sister Rosemary at the Hi-Vee. Let's go, girls. Now! You're stalling. Go kiss Grandma and Grandpa good night."

"Grandpa went to bed," James said.

He found Joe and Eric in the den watching a football game. James watched the game for a few seconds. It looked like Joe Montana was going to take the San Francisco 49ers to the Super Bowl again, his team scoring at will against their cross-bay rivals, the Oakland Raiders. Julie and Rachel were in the living room, drinking cocoa and playing Boggle in front of a blazing fire. James pulled up a chair. Julie was virtually unbeatable at

Boggle, as Rachel was finding out. He waited for the sand in the egg timer to run out.

"You hear about Mike Quinn?" he asked Julie.

"It's so sad," Julie said.

"Do I know Mike Quinn?" Rachel asked.

"He was my best friend growing up. He used to host the post-Christmas white-elephant swap parties."

"The guy in the air force?" Rachel asked. James nodded. "What happened?"

"His helicopter crashed in the desert. I just found out."

"That's awful."

"It is awful," he agreed. He could already feel a kind of protective numbness setting in. "We hadn't stayed in close contact, but still. . . . I don't know what to think." *It must have been his time*, he thought to say. He didn't actually believe in predestination, but it was the sort of thing people said.

"We've been turning the channel at our house when they start talking about the Gulf," Rachel said. "Paul's old enough to understand that some of the boys over there are only eight years older than he is. It's unbelievable how being a parent changes the way you see things."

"I heard someone say they're going to start the whole thing on Christmas Eve because that's the last time anybody would be expecting it."

The fear was that Iraq would use the biological or even nuclear weapons it was thought to possess. No one could begin to guess the number of expected casualties. James knew Mike would have been right there in the thick of things. Perhaps it was best that he'd be spared that.

The grandfather clock chimed in the hall. The timer on the kitchen stove went off, indicating another batch of cookies was done. A roar from the television in the den suggested either the 49ers or the Raiders had scored. Life went on, the small details that added up to a day, days that added inexorably into years. In the living room, the tree had achieved its annual magnificence and glowed cheerfully from the corner of the room.

"Let's not even score this one," Rachel said, rising to her feet and throwing her pad of paper on the table. "You are the undisputed queen of Boggle. Anybody want to help me get those boys of mine into bed?"

"I will in a minute," Julie said. Rachel gathered up the used pieces of paper and threw them into the fireplace.

"Is Dad feeling okay?" James asked. "I saw him on the stairs, and he looked like he was going to be ill."

"Well," Julie said, "I'm not sure. You missed the conversation where Eric announced he's been named president of the bank. They're selling their house and moving to a bigger place where the boys can have their own rooms. Six acres, apparently. In a better school district, big soccer fields, et cetera. It think it took Dad by surprise because they hadn't talked about it before now."

She didn't have to spell it out. The implications were clear. Eric and Rachel were putting down roots in Denver, her hometown, where her family lived. Eric was not going to move back to Onagle to take over the bank, as everyone had long assumed he would. Walter Engler had already announced plans to retire the following summer. Eric's decision didn't give him much time to find a successor. It also left in question what would happen to the house, since their mother had said she wanted to move to their winter getaway in Tucson once their father retired. Suddenly James realized this could be the last Christmas the family spent together here in the house.

"What'd Dad say when Eric told him?"

"'Congratulations,'" Julie said. "What could he say? It was

everything he didn't say. You talked to Sarah?" He nodded. "She still in Hawaii?"

"She moved home. Her dad hasn't been well," James said. "I'm meeting her at the Supper Club."

"Say hi to her for me," Julie said.

"I will," James said.

"I'm sorry about Mike. Some of your friends were a little twerpy, but he was a good kid."

"The best," was all James could say, though it hardly summed it up.

Five

AS HE DROVE TO THE SUPPER CLUB, JAMES REMEM-
bered Mike Quinn, who'd always been a kind of lifeline to his
hometown and his past. James hadn't wanted to go away to
school. Eventually he acclimated to Mill River and accepted his
lot, but he utterly relished coming home for the summer, and he
did his best during the school year to stay in contact with his old
friends, especially Mike and Sarah. He wrote to them whenever
he could, signing his letters "Your Eastern Correspondent." In

his often long and frequently pretentious letters, he painted humorous portraits of prep-school life and drew colorful sketches of his schoolmates.

Michael Quinn was a big, charismatic goofball, confident and affable and a natural leader whom James had more or less idolized. They'd met on the first day of second grade, when the teacher gave them all Tootsie Pops as a treat. When James asked Mike what flavor he'd gotten, he'd opened his mouth and drooled his reply, "Chocolate. You want some?"

Mike was the youngest of five kids, the only boy. His mother and father were both pharmacists, and the fact that they worked until six every day made the Quinn house an ideal after-school hangout. Mike had been the class clown, a star athlete who never struck an elitist jock pose and stayed friendly with kids from all the various cliques, a good-natured boy whom everybody enjoyed being around, with an irrepressible insouciance that made him easy to like. Anytime an animal was mentioned in class, for example, Mike could be counted on to supply the noise it made.

James recalled the time, in fourth grade, when Mike raised his hand and asked the teacher, "Do you think it's fair to punish kids for things they haven't done?"

The teacher, Mrs. Mooney, replied, "Of course not."

"Excellent," Mike said, "because I haven't done my homework."

Mrs. Mooney was known as a disciplinarian, the widow of a man who'd been both the mayor and the editor of the local paper, the *Observer*, a rail-thin woman with a voice gravelly from smoking and an intimidating persona, but she had a bit of a soft spot where "Mr. Quinn" was concerned and usually laughed at his antics in spite of herself. Another time, when Mrs. Mooney told him he had to write "I, Michael Quinn, will not talk in class" one hundred times on the blackboard in an adjacent empty classroom, he instead wrote one hundred times, "Mrs. Mooney is the best teacher in this school and deserves a raise!" How could she be mad?

In high school, Mike moved on to puns and jokes with one-word punch lines, such as, "What's brown and sounds like a bell? Dung," or, "What's brown and sticky? A stick." He also experienced a growth spurt that made him bigger and stronger than most of his peers, though he remained a gentle soul. He played fullback on the football team and ran with great vigor and dash, a smashmouth, head-down, mud-eater of a player, though off the field he showed a sweet disposition and rarely raised his voice in anger.

James remembered working summers at the country club, where he gathered up the gas-powered golf carts when the golfers were finished with them and brought them to Mike at the maintenance shed. Mike in turn refueled and repaired them, having developed the faculty of working with two-stroke engines at an early age by building a succession of go-carts and minibikes, each faster than the one before.

When he was old enough to drive, Mike bought a 1970 Chevelle SS, cherry red with black racing stripes and a black leather interior and ten-inch racing tires and powered by a 350 cubic inch V-8 engine. He detailed the vehicle until it shone, and yet for all the horsepower at his command, he rarely sped or drove recklessly. That wasn't counting the evening of July 4, the summer after they'd graduated from high school, when Mike bet his buddies he could take the car to the railroad crossing west of town and jump it over a pyramid of Leinenkugel six-packs stacked four high. He hit the crossing at ninety miles per hour and cleared the beer by more than a foot. James was not nearly as successful in his father's Audi, bottoming out and damaging the catalytic converter.

James and Mike painted houses the first couple of summers they were home from college, but after their third year, Mike dropped out to join the air force. He had done well enough at Iowa State but had told James on the phone one night that he felt like they were making him learn too much stuff that was never going to do him any good. "I mean seriously, Jimbo, why should I read *Middlemarch*? What reason would anybody have to read *Middlemarch* unless they wanted to get a job teaching English so they could make other people read *Middlemarch*? I'm on page one hundred and so far, that's the only reason I can think of."

At the time Mike enlisted, the various armed forces were all selling themselves in television recruiting advertisements as good places to learn computer or technical skills that would prove valuable later on in civilian life. Later, during the buildup to the Gulf War, there were members of the armed services who claimed such advertisements had misled them and who didn't want to fight. Mike, however, was always proud to serve his country and was eager to get to work on jet planes and giant helicopters.

After his initial training, Mike was sent to David Monthan Air Force Base in Tucson as a mechanic. Promotions came quickly, and before too long he became a chief mechanic, but by then he'd fallen in love with the machines he serviced every day and decided he would do whatever it took to become a pilot. For that, he knew he would need a college degree, so he started attending classes at the University of Arizona during his hours off. When he finished his bachelor's and asked about officer training school, both his immediate superior and the wing commander were more than happy to recommend him. From there he went on to flight training and, finally, just a week before his twenty-fifth birthday, he qualified on the Pavehawk helicopter, the machine he'd been flying when he died.

"These things are like nothing you've ever seen, Jimbo," Mike had told him during a long distance call. "It's like ten thousand rivets, flying in loose formation. Everything shakes so much your fillings fall out. The feeling of raw power is awesome—I don't even want to fly jets."

That was the sort of feeling Mike lived for. His desire for it overwhelmed any awareness he might have had of his own mortality. James remembered telling Mike he was going to die, the night Mike jumped his Chevy over the beer cans.

"Well, you know what the redneck's last four words were, don't you?"

"What?"

"'Hey y'all—watch this!'"

He'd stepped on the gas and driven off in a cloud of dust and a rooster tail of gravel, juiced with the reckless abandon of someone who believed he was going to live forever.

Six

THE ONAGLE SUPPER CLUB (A CLUB IN NAME ONLY) was the best place within a hundred miles to get a filet mignon smothered in mushroom gravy. It was built in the fifties, and the original décor was still intact, including space-age lampshades and vintage beer signs, red Naugahyde-covered booths, and table candles in amber glass globes next to wicker baskets painted gold and holding a variety of individually wrapped crackers. In the sixties the Hilltop Mini-Mall had settled in next to it, financed by the bank. By the time James arrived, plows had already moved the snow into massive piles bordering the shopping center parking lots like mountain ranges, clearing parking spaces for the busiest shopping day of the year.

James entered and noticed that the Supper Club had been decorated for the holidays, with white Christmas lights strung overhead and along the walls, a tree in the corner with fake presents beneath it, and on the wall behind the bar, taped-up paper snowmen with names on them, each snowman representing a customer who'd made a donation to the Toys for Kids fund. Bing Crosby was singing "White Christmas" on the jukebox.

Sarah had gotten a corner booth. He could see her smile from across the room, a sly grin that always had something slightly mischievous about it, even when she'd done nothing mischievous, the twinkle in her eye still there despite the sad occasion. She wore jeans, sneakers, and a gray cashmere sweater. Her light brown hair was pulled back in a ponytail. She smiled weakly when he approached, stood, and extended her arms to hug him. She was clutching a Kleenex in one hand.

"Hi, J.B.," she said. She kissed him on the cheek and lightly rubbed his back. "It's so good to see you. I'd kiss you on the lips, but I don't want you to catch my cold."

She sounded completely stuffed up. She blew her nose. Her eyes were dewy at the corners. She sniffed. "I'm a mess. Sorry."

"We really have to stop meeting like this," he said.

"You can say that again." She sneezed, covering her mouth with the Kleenex. She sort of whooped when she sneezed. Her nose was red.

"Bless you," he said. "I'm sorry I missed your call."

"Well, I'm sorry to have to be the one to tell you. We've all had time to get used to the idea." She sniffed. "It must be a little raw for you."

"I don't know what to say," he said. "It's like I want to know more about what happened, but what good is that going to do?"

"You eat?" she asked. "I'm thinking of picking at the salad bar. Did you know that in restaurants outside of the Midwest, they serve lettuce that isn't iceberg? I was hoping to meet Catherine. Is she here?" She paused. "Uh-oh. I shouldn't have asked. Aw, geez. Forget I said anything."

"It's okay," he said. "Get your salad, and I'll tell you all about it."

"Be right back. Can I get you anything?"

He shook his head and watched her as she walked. The bag she left on the seat beside her was the size of a small duffel bag, but that was Sarah—for as long as he'd known her, she'd always had too much stuff with her.

He smiled when he thought of how familiar she was to him. There was something thoroughly reassuring in that. He remembered how she'd hit him with a Wiffle ball bat in first grade and how he'd nailed her with a water balloon in sixth. He remembered the friendship that had blossomed with maturity and her letters, long and hilarious and free of misspellings or grammatical errors, handwritten on unruled stationery, using a straightedge to keep her lines straight.

"Cheer up, Otis—I have every confidence that one day you will make some girl very happy," she'd once written. "Unfortunately, most girls need more than one day." How excited he'd been to find her letters in his mailbox at college. On one occasion, he'd unintentionally made a girlfriend jealous by reading one of Sarah's letters out loud.

Sarah hadn't much liked UCLA, or Los Angeles, and had moved to Honolulu after she'd graduated for the chance to manage an upscale clothing store there. In Hawaii, she'd met Kevin, who worked for the Hilton hotel chain. When Kevin took a job in Bangkok and Sarah went with him, she wrote to James, "Will keep you posted as best I can. If I get sacrificed to a volcano or something, remember me to those I love."

"We don't have to talk about it, you know," she said when she got back. "If you don't want to. I didn't mean to pry."

"You're not prying," he told her. "As I recall, we promised each other once that we could talk about anything." He remembered meeting with Mike and Sarah in this very restaurant, making big plans about how they were going to get out of this town and what they were going to do with their lives when they did.

"What's wrong?" Sarah asked. "You look like you just thought of something."

"I'm not trying to be evasive," he said. "I was thinking about what to say while you were getting your salad, but I couldn't come up with anything. I wasn't feeling so good before I got home, and now with Mike. . . ." He realized how much he'd been holding his feelings back. In the company of Sarah, he felt safe to let them out.

"I know," she said. "Almost makes you want to cry, doesn't it?"

She handed him a Kleenex. He dried the tear that was rolling down his cheek.

"Almost," he said, but there were more where that one came from. Sarah's eyes were wet as well. For a moment, he let the tears come. He drew a deep breath, blew his nose, and dried his eyes again. Embarrassed, he covered his eyes with his hand, lowered his head, and drew another deep breath. She took his other hand and squeezed it.

"I'm not all that fond of weeping in public, to tell the truth," he said, looking around to see if anyone was watching. No one was.

"There's nothing wrong with crying, you know," she said. "Lots of people do it."

"I know," he said. "It just doesn't seem right to sit here feeling sorry for myself." He thought of Mike's family.

"This isn't feeling sorry for yourself," she told him. "You're entitled."

"Thanks," he told her, blowing his nose and drying his eyes one last time. He'd always appreciated the moral clarity she brought to their discussions, an emotional orderliness that had helped him keep things in perspective.

"Get your Christmas shopping done yet?" she asked. He was glad to change the subject, though he knew they'd circle back to it. She nibbled at her plate of ripe olives and pickled beets, croutons, and feta cheese. "The line to Santa's castle at the Mini-Mall is manageable after nine if you want to go sit on his lap." She looked down and sniffed. "This salad looks good, but I can barely taste anything."

"Since when did Santa live in a castle?" James asked. "I thought he was one of us. What's he king of?"

"The Hilltop Mini-Mall, I guess. You know what you're getting people?"

"Books for the grown-ups and something fun for the kids," he said. "This is what we do, isn't it?"

"What?"

"Just keep going," he said. "Buy presents, business as usual. Pick up a gallon of milk on the way home from the funeral, talk about the weather, feed the dog. . . ." He thought of Cully's words: *Sometimes you do stuff just 'cause it's stuff you always do.* "Act like everything's normal until everything is normal."

"That's what we do," she agreed. "It's more heroic than it looks. I used to get so angry at Kevin for being so stubborn—

obnoxious, sometimes—but that's how some people survive, I guess."

"How is Kevin?" he asked, though by the way she brought him up, he was pretty sure he already knew the answer.

"Out of the picture." She fought off a false sneeze for a few moments, then blew her nose again. He waited.

"Since?"

"Since we moved to Bangkok and he started partying every night with the Eurotrash hippies and the Sultan of Brunei's nephews and doing all kinds of things he shouldn't have. Though we waited until we were back in Hawaii before we really broke up."

"I'm sorry," James said.

"He claimed he was just schmoozing them up because he wanted them to invest in a restaurant we were going to open in Honolulu. They taught him that in business school. Schmooze or lose."

"Did you?"

"Schmooze?"

"Open a restaurant."

"I didn't," she said. "He did. I'd had enough. He barely lasted six months."

"How come?"

"Well," she said, "I don't know for sure, but I think he made two mistakes." She held up two fingers to enumerate. "First, he assumed all the friends he'd met through the Hilton were going to eat in his restaurant every night, and they didn't. Second, he thought he could sleep with all his waitresses and do drugs with them in the basement and still keep the business running." She wiggled her two fingers, then rotated her hand while lowering her pointer finger. "Technically we were still involved when I found that out," she said.

"Yikes," James said. "How'd you find out?"

"The sous-chef was a friend. But enough about me. How's your work going? I keep looking for you in the *New Yorker*."

"Don't hold your breath," he told her.

"Are you still in school?"

"One more semester."

"Ph.D.?"

"M.F.A."

"Do you like it?"

"The teachers are great," he said, "if you can ever get an appointment to see one. Most of the time they're off being writers in New York."

"Is that what you want to be?"

"I'd like to be successful some day," he said. "Maybe not in New York. I think we just broke our own record for crime. Dinkins can't even keep the garbage collected. I wouldn't mind moving if I had a good place to go." He chose not to mention the emotional turmoil that had stopped him from writing much the past year and the pressure he'd felt trying to follow up on the story he'd published in the *New Yorker*.

"So what are your dreams?" she asked him.

"My dreams?"

"Yeah, J.B. Your dreams. Give 'em up. I know you got 'em."

"I don't know," he said. "The usual."

"If it's the usual, it's not a dream."

"That depends on where you're starting from. You know what I really want? What I really want is just time. I know it sounds corny, but I wish I had time to just write, and whether it got published would be beside the point. The part I like is just the writing, losing myself in stories. If I had the time to do that without worrying about paying the rent, I think I'd be happy."

"Well, you could start by writing me letters again. You know,

I saved all the ones you wrote me from college. I figured one day you'd be famous and then I could sell 'em and cash in."

"You're kidding, right?"

"Got 'em in a notebook," she said. "In chronological order. Last I checked. It's not like I take 'em out every night to read."

"I'm sure they were completely idiotic," he said, laughing even though he felt genuinely touched. "As I recall, that was back when I thought I knew all the answers. Now I don't even understand the questions."

"Well, then, that's progress," she told him. "Who wants to read somebody who knows all the answers?"

He smiled.

"Mill River said they were looking to add a writing instructor."

"They called you?" she said. "That's great. Are you going to do it?"

"I don't know," he said. "Did you ever read *Middlemarch*?"

"No, why?"

"Nothing," he said. "Just thinking out loud."

"I wouldn't knock teaching," she said. "At least you know you're doing somebody some real good. What does Catherine think about that option? Oops. Sorry. I wasn't going to bring her up."

"It's okay. For the first three years, they make you live in a dorm. She wasn't big on that," he said. "You're basically on duty round-the-clock. To tell you the truth, she just wasn't so big on me anymore either. We've called the engagement off."

"Oh, no," she said. "I figured something was wrong when you didn't say anything about her on the phone. Where are you with it? And don't be flippant like you usually get."

"I'm not sure," he said. "Honestly. I know you can't go back, but I'm not sure how to go forward either. My buddy in New York says, 'Move on, it's over,' but it's not so cut and dried. You know? You can't tell yourself how to feel. You just try to let it all flow through you—I sound like some guru."

"What happened? Can you say? We don't have to talk about it if you don't want to."

"Got all night?"

"Long as you want."

"I can't put it in a nutshell. We stopped connecting. I think she thought our life would be easier. Most of her friends have a lot more security than I can offer her. Living in New York on a teaching assistant's stipend didn't leave much left over for the finer things. It's been a real struggle financially. We were always fighting about money and what we could or couldn't afford to do."

She shook her head.

"You know that wasn't the real problem, right?" Sarah said, leaning in. "There's not a couple alive that doesn't fight about money, and as far as I can tell, it makes no difference whether you're flat broke or rich as Rockefeller. If you really love someone, you can live with them in a shoebox."

"I suppose," he said.

"It sounds to me like she just wasn't very mature," Sarah said. "I don't know her, but it just doesn't sound like she was seeing the real you. Like she was just looking for all the ways you could change. Doesn't that make you angry? That would make me *so* angry. I forgot—you said you don't get angry."

He remembered what his sister had said about blame. The fact was, it was hard to be angry at Catherine when, if he were to truly take responsibility for his failures, it seemed like he had only himself to blame. The fact was, there'd been a time, back when they'd first gotten engaged, when they could have marched right into a justice of the peace's office and done the deed. Catherine had wanted to. He'd been the one who'd lost his nerve. When she asked him what he was waiting for, he'd been unable to tell her because he knew only that he was afraid, afflicted with "cold feet" *in extremis* almost from the moment they'd agreed to marry. He knew he'd been trying to protect himself, but from what? He told her he needed—and he couldn't believe what a cliché he was being—more space, more time. She'd been patient at first, but her patience had eventually worn thin.

"I'm angry at myself, I guess," he said.

"So let me ask you this," she said. "If you had a time machine, would you go forward or backward?"

"Hmm," he said. "That's a good question."

"The way I see it, that's the only question."

"I don't know how to answer it," he told her. "How about you? Been dating anyone?"

She gave him a look that said she knew he was changing the subject, then shook her head.

"I am so over dating," she said.

"Well, you don't want to over-date," he said.

"Don't even start. Plus, in case you haven't noticed," she glanced around the room furtively, whispering, "I live *here* now. Onagle's not exactly teeming with eligible bachelors."

James scanned the room as if searching for Sarah's perfect partner. At the bar, a very large man in overalls and a feed cap was eating buffalo wings, bones and all. James nodded toward the man, but Sarah shook her head.

"How about Ben Larson?" James asked. "Isn't he still around?"

"Chicago," she said. "Though I suspect he's home for the holidays. Anyway, he's not in the picture."

"Julie said they got more snow in Chicago than they did here."

"Can you keep a secret?" Sarah said. "No, of course not; you never could, but I'm telling you anyway. Seriously, I'm thinking long and hard about becoming a single mom."

"Really?"

"Yup. The bad part is, you don't have anybody there to help you, but the good part is, you don't have anybody there to 'help' you."

"Are you talking about adopting?" he asked.

"That's one option," she said. "There are others."

"Kidnapping?"

"Others."

"Wow," he said. "Huh."

"What do you mean, 'huh'?"

"Well, nothing," he said. "I just figured you always liked guys chasing you—you just didn't like them catching you."

"What's that supposed to mean?"

"Well," he said, "I just mean how you flirted with me and chased after me ever since we were little, trying to get me to chase you back."

"Not."

"Too."

"I absolutely did not."

"You absolutely did too."

"In your dreams."

"You're right. You absolutely did not," he said. "I must have imagined the whole twenty years. I'll be right back."

Seven

WHEN JAMES RETURNED FROM THE BATHROOM, he saw that Sarah had been joined by two more old friends, Terry and Martha. In a town the size of Onagle, with so few places to go, it was inevitable that you'd run into somebody if you stayed in one place long enough. It was one of the things James liked about coming home. He'd wondered if he would see these two, who had gotten married since he last saw them. He'd been surprised when his mother wrote to tell him about the wedding and then, later, about the babies. He hadn't even known Terry and Martha were dating.

Sarah excused herself and said now she had to go to the ladies' room.

"Just for the record," she told James before she left, "I don't want you to chase me."

"What'd she mean by that?" Martha asked as Sarah walked away.

Martha was Pastor Gruening's daughter, and a typical preacher's kid. In James's experience, there were only two ways a P.K. could go, either walking the straight and narrow or headed for hell in a handbasket, as his mother might have said. Martha had chosen the latter path, for a while, anyway, having earned a bit of a reputation in her wilder years. It was strange to think of her as married.

"Nothing," James said. "I was just telling Sarah how she's had the hots for me for years."

"You wish," Terry said. "I tried setting her up with a buddy of mine a few months ago, but she shot him down cold."

"It's none of our business," Martha said, elbowing him play-fully. "Besides, I know a guy in Ames who's just right for her."

"One of your old boyfriends, no doubt," Terry said, turning to James. "Martha has this fantasy that the guys she dumped are going to pine away over her forever unless she sets them up with somebody else." Terry gave her a grin as she stuck out her tongue at him.

Terry Kesler had taken over a farm started by his grandfather and lost it in 1987 after borrowing thirty-five thousand dollars to build a storage bin for his grain. When everything crashed, the bank had called in the loan, and when Terry refused to pay another dime beyond the original agreement, they'd gotten a court order and sent a crew to repossess the bin, only to find it smashed to pieces. Terry had repeatedly driven his tractor into it in a drunken rage, earning him a month in jail. The bin had gone away, but the drunkenness and the rage hadn't—at least not by the last time James had seen him. Now, James noticed, Terry was drinking only coffee.

"So how've you been?" James asked. "I missed seeing you last year. How's married life?"

"With two kids under the age of two?" Martha said. "You kiddin' me? This is the first time we've been out on a date since last summer."

"Don't let me wreck it," James offered. "If you guys want to be alone—"

"No way, man," Terry said. "Good to see you."

"Keeping busy?" James asked. "Still fixing stuff? I know the economy's been pretty rough."

"Yeah, but that's good for me," Terry said. "Worse it gets, the more people repair things instead of replace 'em. How about you? Still out east?"

James nodded. He watched Terry add three Sweet'N Lows to his coffee cup and stir the contents.

"So far, so good," James lied.

"That was so terrible about Mike," Martha said. As she spoke, she removed a sweater she was knitting from the bag she'd carried in. "I'm trying to finish this before Christmas," she explained. "Anyway, it's really true what they say about the good dying young, isn't it? Did Sarah tell you we're still having the party?" James nodded again. "Everybody's going to say something, so think about what you want to say."

"I'm still getting up to speed on all this," James said. "I just found out today."

Martha fished in her pocketbook and handed James a photocopy of the local newspaper article describing the tragedy. James scanned the details. Mike had been stationed at Eglin Air Force Base in Fort Walton Beach, Florida. His unit had been sent to the Gulf in October, operating out of an undisclosed location in Saudi Arabia. He'd been flying an HH60 Pavehawk helicopter, training for rescue work. The article said that he was survived by his parents and his sisters.

Sarah rejoined them. She looked at Martha.

"You bring your knitting on a date?" she asked.

Terry looked to the ceiling.

"I can party and knit at the same time," Martha said defensively. "That's all my knitting circle does when we go to Okoboji—knit and drink strawberry daiquiris. We call it Stitch 'N' Bitch. You have to come with us next summer."

Sarah smiled politely.

"Was he with anybody?" James asked. "Mike, I mean. Did he have a girlfriend or anybody like that?"

"Not that we know," Sarah said. "When was the last time you saw him?"

"It would have been two years ago, I guess. Right after Christmas. He called me up and asked me if I wanted to go shoot pool. He was all excited about becoming a pilot. I don't remember much more than that."

This was not true. He did remember more than that.

"At least he died doing something he loved," Martha said, her knitting needles pausing. "You know, if you think about it, that's such a stupid thing to say. Wouldn't it be better to die doing something you hate? Then at least you don't have to do it any more."

"When my brother died," James said, "people kept telling me he was doing what he loved, and I just wanted to scream at them. It made no sense to me."

Sarah rubbed his hand beneath the table.

"Mrs. Mooney said something like that," Sarah said. "She said one of life's riddles is how something that happens every day, and comes to all of us sooner or later, so often doesn't make sense, even though it's human nature to try to make sense of it. I liked that she didn't try to explain it. She called it 'life's great ambiguity.' I remember because I went home and looked the word *ambiguity* up in the dictionary."

"I don't remember her saying that," James said.

"You weren't there. It was the day before your brother's

funeral. You were still out of school. She was trying to explain to the class what had happened to Gerry and what a funeral was. I think that was the first funeral I ever went to."

"Me too," James said.

"She was a real good teacher," Terry said. "A little frightening, but good."

"She still is," Martha said. "My nieces have her."

"She's still teaching?" James asked. "She must be two thousand years old."

"Yeah, but that's good for teaching history," Sarah said. "I think she actually dated Robert E. Lee."

They chatted about old times and what they remembered about Mike until Terry looked at his watch and said it was getting late. He scraped his empty Sweet'N Low envelopes into a pile; he'd used at least twenty in the hour they'd been talking. James looked at the clock behind the bar. It was ten-thirty. In New York City, people would just be going out to eat at that hour.

Sarah went to the pay phone to call her mother to tell her she was coming home and to ask her if there was anything they needed from the Qwik Trip, while Terry went to pay his bill. James took the opportunity to ask Martha a question. "Confidentially," he said, "is Sarah serious about being a single mom? Has she really given up on men?"

"Sarah has dated two kinds of guys her whole life," Martha said, moving her lips as she counted her stitches to cast off before putting her knitting away. "Either they're, like, really good-looking, stupid guys who aren't her equal and leave her feeling empty, or they're guys who are more stubborn than she is and they end up fighting all the time. The only guy she ever really got along with was you, and that's just because you were never interested."

"Cream for the cat," Sarah said, returning from the phone. James wore a puzzled expression. "I asked her what she needed, and that's what she said. The cat's big as a sow already, but what the heck. Maybe I'll get her eggnog."

James walked Sarah to her car over packed snow that squeaked underfoot. Sometimes you could tell how cold it was just from the sound the snow made when you walked on it. Sarah walked slowly, hands stuffed into her pockets.

"It's kinda hard to get in the Christmas spirit this year," she said. "Thinking about Mike and everything else."

James nodded. "It's terrible," he said. "The world needs more people like him, not fewer. I mean, there's so many whiny malcontents who suck the life out of everything. Like me. And then there's people like Mike who add their energy and their spirit to the world just by being here. I'm not putting it very succinctly."

"I know what you mean," she said. "And you're not a whiny malcontent."

"He made it a better place."

"On that note, Merry Christmas," she said. "Give your family a big hug from me. I see your mom around. Not your dad so much. How are they handling the thing with Catherine?"

"Well," James said, "they were going to have a party for us, but I guess that's not going to happen."

"I know," Sarah said. "That's what I was referring to. They called me about that. Your mom did."

"What did she say?"

"She said they were going to have to reschedule."

"I guess that's easier than telling people they were canceling it outright. I think in their eyes we were already married," James said. "I guess, to some people, living together would seem to be the same thing. But it's not."

"You don't have to tell me," Sarah said.

"Anyway, see you tomorrow night—you still go to the candlelight service, don't you?"

"That's the plan," she said.

She hugged him again and kissed him on the cheek, up near his ear. She smelled familiar to him. He felt a warmth coming from her body, even through the heavy winter coat she wore. As he held her, she sneezed one last time.

"Take some echinacea or something," he told her.

"Doesn't work for me," she said. "My doctor said hot fudge sundaes would be good."

"Well, then listen to your doctor."

On his way home, he passed the bowling alley where he and Mike had shot pool. Mike had beaten him five games in a row playing eightball. They'd talked mostly about the air force and Mike's new opportunity to fly helicopters. "They're paying me to do what other people pay to do," Mike said. "How can that be a bad thing?" James tried to tell him what he did was dangerous, but Mike wouldn't hear it. He had his whole life mapped out. He was going to fly helicopters for the air force for as long as he could and retire on a fat military pension and then fly medivac helicopters for hospitals.

"Suit yourself," James had said, "but if you crash, I'm not coming to your funeral."

Eight

HE DROVE HOME THROUGH THE FAMILIAR STREETS of his hometown. Though it was slightly out of his way, he drove past the Larsons' home. The house was brightly lit, electric candles in the windows, white holiday lights trimming the eaves, colored lights glittering in the trees and bushes, and a shining wreath fastened to the front door, its red ribbon reaching nearly to the ground. Cars overflowed the driveway and lined up down the block. By the front walk, somebody had built a snowman holding a cardboard sign that said *"God Jul."*

At home he found his mother still busy in the kitchen, cutting out more sugar cookies. Everyone else appeared to have gone to bed. As a teen, whenever James stayed out past curfew, launching automobiles off railroad crossings or helping Mike vandalize some rival high school's bus with spray paint, his mother had been the one who had waited up to call him on the carpet. In a completely benign way, it felt familiar to see her still up and puttering about.

"How was your night?" she asked. "I'm still so sorry about Michael. It's such a shame."

"I know," he said.

"Everything happens for a reason," she said. He knew she believed that.

"Well . . ." was all he could manage.

"How's Sarah?" she asked. "I know Tom's been having problems with the VA hospital."

"Sarah's good, I guess," he said, knowing that, in a town the size of Onagle, he could be sure his mother already knew the reasons why Sarah moved home. "It's always so easy to talk to her. No matter how long it's been, we always pick up where we left off. We ran into Terry and Martha. He looked great. When did he quit drinking?"

"I'm not sure, exactly," she said, nodding him toward a little collection of broken cookies at the corner of the table, bidding him to take one, "but I know at their wedding they only served apple cider. Everyone had just as good a time as they would have if they'd served alcohol. Doesn't that just say something?" She carefully transferred another shape to the baking sheet.

"Do you really need more cookies?" James asked. "You should relax."

"Just sugar cookies," she said. "The kids love them, and I'd hate to run out."

"Can I help?"

She smiled. "You can do the sprinkles."

"All red or all green?" he asked, taking up the McCormick sprinkles jars, one in each hand.

"Make a few all red because Abigail likes those, but other than that, I'll leave it up to you."

She looked at him, studying him a moment.

"Your hair is getting so much darker."

"It's not, Mom. You say that every time I come home."

"I know, but I just can't get over how much darker it is."

"What do you think of Eric's toupee?" James asked. "Kind of startling, isn't it?"

"I think it's just fine, if that's what he wants," she said. "He had more hair on the day he was born than he has now. You know your Grandma Helen wore a wig. Why do you ask, though? What do you think of it?"

"I think it looks good," James said. "But then I thought he looked good bald. And I especially thought he looked good bald whenever I was standing next to him not bald."

"Oh, you," she said. She touched his hair to see how thin it was getting. "Tell me—is now a good time? I wanted to talk to you. Your father and I don't want to pry, but we were sorry when we found out Catherine wouldn't be joining us."

He'd been waiting for this. He knew he could count on his mother to bring it up, as much as he could count on his father to avoid it. He was tired of telling the story, though—especially to himself.

"I know, Mom," he said. "I'm really sorry I didn't say something before. I know you were planning on having a party for us, and I want to reimburse you for any expenses because I know I should have called before you went to the trouble."

"Oh, Jimmy, don't even think about that. That's not important. We just want you to be happy." She took her apron off and hung it from a hook in the pantry. She took a bottle from a high shelf. "I'm having a glass of sherry. Can I get you one?"

"I'm fine," James said, slipping a chipped tree-shaped sugar cookie into his mouth whole.

"There's eggnog in the refrigerator," his mother said. "And fresh nutmeg." He was about to decline, but the offer of fresh nutmeg was too tempting to refuse. She poured him a large glass. He grated the seed over the glass, the aroma wafting up sweet and ancient. It was such a wonderful smell. He wondered why people only used the spice during the holidays.

"So your father and I wanted to know—is there anything we can do?" his mother asked, joining him at the kitchen table.

"I can't imagine what."

"Would it help if we wrote Catherine a letter?"

"Saying what?" he asked, more out of curiosity than hope.

"Well, I don't know exactly what I'd say, but I know your father and I had to learn a few things to make it as far as we have.

We learned never to go to bed angry, and maybe that's not very original, but that doesn't make it any less true. If you have something that's bothering you, you stay up and talk it through."

"I know you feel that way," James said, having heard the speech about never going to bed angry any number of times before. "What do you do, though, when you talk and talk and you never get anywhere? Because that's the way it is with us."

"Maybe you're not talking for the right reasons," his mother said, sipping from her small finger glass. "You don't talk to get the other person to say uncle, you know. You don't argue until the other person says, 'I give up, I'm wrong, you're right, you win.' And you don't hammer away until the other person sees your point of view. You ask questions until you see *each other's* point of view. It only works if you both do it. You talk *with* each other, not *at* each other. You listen without thinking up what you're going to say next. You *listen*."

He paused a moment, staring straight at her, then shook his head as if to wake himself from a daydream.

"I'm sorry, what were you saying?"

His joke made her smile.

"You kid, but I know you know what I'm saying."

"That's hard for some people to do," he said.

"That's hard for *everybody* to do," she told him. "Have you thought about counseling?"

"We've been to counseling," he said, growing desperate to change the subject. "It didn't help."

"So where did you leave it?"

"Well," he said, not knowing what to say, "I guess if something doesn't change soon, it's over. And I'm not sure what that something could be. I'm sorry I can't be more helpful than that."

He knew that, in his parents' world, giving up was not an option. He couldn't tell her how much faith he'd lost because he'd thought Catherine was the one for him and he'd been wrong, so how could he ever be sure again? He couldn't tell her how dark his dark moments were of late—about the black, hollow feeling he'd been fighting since Thanksgiving, a deep and abiding despair unlike anything he'd known before, a deep sense of worthlessness that went away during the day but returned at night.

"Do you think it would have helped if you'd had a bit more . . . security? Financial, I mean."

"It's hard to say. Maybe." He changed the subject. "Did you

hear they're going ahead with the party for Mike? Tuesday night, after the memorial. Everybody's figuring he wouldn't mind if we threw him one last party."

It was egocentric of him, but he wondered all the same if his telling Mike he wasn't coming to his funeral had anything to do with Mike's asking not to have one. Probably not. More likely, Mike didn't want any official gathering of gloom in his name because it wasn't in his nature to be gloomy.

"I did hear that," his mother said. "I dropped off a casserole and told Carol Quinn if she wanted to talk, to give me a call. Not that there's much I could say that would help. I know they decided against Arlington."

"Last time I saw him, we were shooting pool, and I told him if he died, I wasn't coming to his funeral. How do you like that?"

"Well, you couldn't have known," his mother said. "People say things like that all the time."

He'd arranged all the broken cookies together on a plate. He pushed it toward his mother. She said, "Well, maybe just one more," and proceeded to eat three. They tasted, to James, like childhood. He supposed they tasted the same to his mother. How much could sugar cookies have changed since she was young?

She was quick to sweep up any spilled crumbs, using the side of her hand and depositing the spilled crumbs in the wastebasket.

"What do you remember from the last time you saw Gerry?" he asked. They'd never talked about this before. He wondered why not. "Do you remember?"

"Well, he'd been home for Christmas, but he got called back early. He was going to stay until New Year's Eve, but then he couldn't. So before he left, we had chow mein from Hong Kong Gardens because that was his favorite. What do you remember?"

"I remember we had a fight," James said. "Though for the life of me, I can't remember what it might have been about."

"It probably wasn't about anything," she told him. She crossed to the refrigerator as she spoke, where she filled her empty sherry glass with eggnog from the carton. "That was your way of dealing with it."

"With what?"

"With the stress. And the worry." She drained her glass, then stepped over to the sink and rinsed it. "You were old enough by then to understand what was going on in the world, but I don't think you were old enough to express what you were feeling, so you acted out."

"I did?"

"You acted out every time Gerry left. First you'd run away and storm off in a big pout, and then you'd come back mad."

"Why?"

"Well, I'm not quite sure, but I know you watched the news a lot, so you knew where he was going. You knew what Vietnam was. You didn't understand it fully, but you knew it was danger-ous, I think, so you were concerned. But you didn't know how to say that, so you got mad instead."

He'd thought often about what his last words to his brother had been. He couldn't remember what they'd fought about, but he clearly remembered saying, in all his nine-year-old rage, "I hope you never come back!"

Nine

JAMES DROVE TO THE MINI-MALL THE NEXT DAY TO finish his shopping. There were only a dozen stores to choose from, with a Sears at one end and a K-Mart at the other, but he made do. He got Kirstin (who'd asked her mother if she could shave her head) a Sinéad O'Connor "Nothing Compares 2 U" lunchbox and found a *Little Mermaid* wallet for Abigail. For Paul and Thomas, he bought matching Denver Broncos football jerseys with John Elway's name and number on them, and for

Henry, a battery-operated parrot that could record and play back whatever you said to it. He spent an hour at B. Dalton's picking out books—an art book for Julie, a gardening book for Lisa, a book on World War I for his father, a cookbook for his mother, a thriller for Joe, a golf book for Eric.

When he got home, Abigail, Kirstin, Paul, Thomas, and Henry were returning from the lake in the center of town, where Joe and Eric had taken them ice skating. Paul and Thomas had brought along hockey sticks. Little Henry had used a frame made out of plastic PVC piping to help him skate without falling, pushing it ahead of him on the ice. Kirstin had learned some figure skating moves and had white puffballs on the laces of her skates, which, according to Joe, Abigail envied terribly. The kids were all excited about Christmas Eve, in the uncomplicated way that kids could get excited. James spent the afternoon playing with his nieces and nephews, hoping some of that innocence would rub off on him.

"Is Aunt Catherine coming *today?*" Abigail sang out at one point.

"No, she's not coming today. She's with her mommy and daddy and the rest of her family."

"I got her a present," his niece said.

"That's very nice of you. I'll make sure that she gets it. I'm sure she'll love it."

The house smelled of wood smoke from the fireplace, pine boughs, turkey and stuffing, scented candles, and spiced apple cider, a heady suffusion of holiday aromas. Julie, Rachel, and Lisa were in the den. His father was stringing lights along the eaves on the front of the house, an unusually last-minute job for him. James looked out the window and watched his father work. Christmas was more important to the old man than it was to anybody else in the family. James had once remarked about that to his mother.

"Well, you know," she'd said, "don't tell him I told you this, but I think it's because he was always so homesick when he went away to school. You were too, but I think your father was worse, being the oldest and the first to go from his generation. He said he was really quite unhappy for a long time, but he couldn't tell anyone because he'd been taught not to complain. You know how he is. But he was so glad each year to come home for the holidays."

James understood that his father was not very good at talking about his feelings and therefore depended on the annual repetition of holiday rituals and ceremonies to reassure him that

everything was okay because nothing had changed. He remembered the arguments they'd had, particularly after he'd turned, at
the age of fourteen, into a knee-jerk leftist radical opposed to all
foreign military interventions, no matter what the justification,
while his father remained a staunch Republican who supported
his government and its military and loved his country right or
wrong. "It's like you don't even remember what happened to
Gerry," young James had shouted in one of his worst moments.

Their political arguments had escalated after the election of
Ronald Reagan, a man Walter Engler considered one of the finer
presidents America had ever had. "He hasn't read a book since
1961," James had argued, home from his second year at Brown
and full of an English major's lofty opinions about literature. "His
favorite poet is Robert W. Service, for God's sake!" This argument
was lost on his father, who liked the bouncy cadences of the old
Yukon storyteller too. At one time in his life, Walter had even
committed "The Shooting of Dan McGrew" to memory.

As might have been expected, the more mature James
became, the more he recognized he'd unfairly judged his father,
who wasn't mean or hardhearted in any way. He was reserved
only because when his feelings were stirred up, he preferred to

sit back and observe them with as much detachment as possible, to get a more useful perspective—a habit James had begun to recognize in himself. James's father also confused sympathy with empathy and believed that thinking about someone else's problem and asking himself, "What would I do in that situation?" was the same thing as understanding their experience of it. He was intelligent and self-reflective to the extent that each night in his prayers he asked God to help him see his faults more clearly, but his attempts at understanding others, especially his children, were often stabs in the dark.

James got it, largely because he knew he wasn't exactly a gifted empathizer either and that the apple had not fallen so far from the tree where emotional understanding was concerned. He knew his father loved him as best he could, in his own way, based on how he'd been taught to love by the generations before him. Watching his father through the window, James wished there were some way to bridge the gap between them. The arguments had ended years ago. Why did the distance remain?

IN THE ENGLER FAMILY, CHRISTMAS WAS CELEBRATED on the evening of the twenty-fourth, with the traditional feast coming on Christmas Eve. The fires were lit at noon, one in the den fireplace and one in the living room. The boys in the family usually spent part of the morning hauling in enough firewood to last the day. Appetizers were set out in the early afternoon— bowls of roasted chestnuts, pistachios, heavy dark rye breads and baguettes, strange Scandinavian smoked goat cheeses and soft triple-cream French cheeses and exotic crackers from tins, smoked mussels, delicate porcelain bowls of beluga caviar, pickled herring, smoked herring paste, lingonberry relish, and boxes of Swiss and German chocolates and old-fashioned American ribbon candy. Ruth Engler was obliged by custom to warn people no fewer than a dozen times not to ruin their appetites by overindulging in appetizers.

The stereo was always kept tuned to WHO out of Des Moines, the station that played Christmas music all day long, interrupted only to rerun the classic radio version of Dickens's *A Christmas Carol* at three. People were free to do as they pleased until four, when it was time to go upstairs and clean up and get ready. Males over the age of eight were expected to wear coats and ties. Females dressed commensurately, generally wearing dresses or skirts. Julie had been the first to wear slacks a few years back, but they had been part of an elegant black suit she'd bought for job interviews and met with her father's approval.

Dinner was served at five o'clock. The centerpiece this year, as always, was a spectacular display of poinsettias, holly, mistletoe, juniper, wheat, bittersweet, and seasonal berries from Lisa's yard and greenhouse, artfully composed by James's oldest sister, who as a girl had taken home a series of blue ribbons for her floral arrangements and hadn't lost her touch.

True to the family's Norwegian heritage, *lutefisk* (cod preserved in lye) and *lefse* (versatile potato crepes served buttered and sugared) were part of the menu, but the rest was pure Midwestern America. The table sagged under dishes of turkey, goose, mashed potatoes and gravy, wild rice, rice pudding, sweet potatoes, stuffing, creamed corn, broccoli in a cream sauce, and sautéed green beans with bread crumbs. There were cranberry relish, cranberry sauce, cranberry juice, cranberry chutney, cranberry bread, and a cranberry-free *julekake* for Joe (who was allergic to cranberries), plus applesauce, cottage cheese, and *fruktsuppe,* a warm fruit compote made from raisins, peaches, and tapioca. (Eric had adopted a new diet regimen and passed on much of this.) Dessert was served as soon as the dinner plates were cleared. It consisted of pumpkin pie, pecan pie, apple pie, a dozen different kinds of (unbroken) cookies, *rommegrøt, kransekake, krumkake, kringle,* spumoni ice cream (for the holiday colors), and pitted dates.

There was an hour-long break between dessert and the recommencement of festivities, during which time the grand-children were expected to go upstairs and plan some sort of Christmas program. Usually they selected carols, and sometimes they wrote skits or created dances, but there were no rules as long as the performance had something to do with Christmas.

It was during this break that James's father asked him if they could talk for a minute in his study. Dinner conversation had skirted any number of unpleasant subjects—the pending Gulf War, the banking crisis, and the Larson's party—and stuck to things like how the kids were doing in school, what was wrong with the Minnesota Vikings ("I miss Bud Grant, even though he couldn't win a Super Bowl, either," Joe said), the new airport in Denver ("From a distance," Eric said, "it looks like the world's largest ice cream parlor"), Lisa's thoughts about building a greenhouse for their mother, or Julie's success with a new gallery near Navy Pier.

The only reference to Catherine's absence, as far as James

noticed, had come during the saying of grace. "We are grateful for the love of those present and for those who could not be present," his father had said, "and we ask that you bless all those who aren't with us tonight."

In the den, his father gestured for James to have a seat on the couch. Walter sat down in his reading chair. He was wearing his red Christmas bow tie, but otherwise he looked every bit the banker. It was in this den, in these chairs, that James's father had conducted many a moral lesson, financial lecture, investigative hearing, or disciplinary action during James's childhood. James found it hard not to feel apprehensive.

"I wanted to talk to you about Catherine," his father said.

"Okay," James said. "She did ask me to give her apologies and said she hoped everybody would understand."

"Well, I'm not sure that I do," his father said, "but your mother and I just wanted you to know we're sorry because we both like Catherine, and it makes us sad when our kids are sad. It was actually Julie who suggested I talk to you, but I guess I don't know what to say about these things. I don't have much experience. I feel bad about that."

"Don't," James said. "It's all just part of the process."

"So would you say this is some kind of cooling-off period?" his father asked.

"Well," James said, "it's not exactly a cooling-off period. Things are pretty cold."

The word *arctic* came to mind.

"But there's nothing final or irreversible yet. Is that right?"

"I guess not," James said, wondering what his father was getting at. "There's always hope, right?"

"I know I'm groping in the dark," James's father said. "Maybe there's a better way to say this, but I think I'll just blunder ahead anyway, and forgive me if I sound indelicate. I was talking to your mother, and we thought maybe there's a way we could help. I gather there's some financial strain involved in the troubles the two of you are having."

"No more than with most couples, I think," James said. "Most graduate students, anyway."

"To be blunt," his father continued, "I gather you feel success is something you'll achieve . . . later on, rather than now. Is that correct?"

"Well," James said, "I guess it depends on what you mean by success."

"I'm not trying to criticize. I only mean that you seem to be on a long-term plan. You're willing to wait ten or fifteen years if that's what it takes to get a teaching job or get a book published. I understand that some writers become overnight successes, but the majority have to develop their craft over time, and many don't really achieve success until their forties or fifties. Is that correct?"

James realized his father had been looking out for him, in his own way, by doing research, getting the facts and analyzing them. He must have read an article somewhere about how long it took some writers to establish their careers. The fact that he assumed James had some sort of plan made James want to smile.

"I haven't really thought about how long it could take," James said, though this wasn't quite true. "That part's out of my control. But I suppose, yeah, I'm willing to do this for as long as it takes."

"And teaching is part of your plan?"

"It wasn't," James said, "but I did get a letter from Mill River saying they might be opening up an instructor's position. My old teacher there recommended me. It wouldn't pay much, but they make the new teachers live in the dorms for the first few years, so food and housing would be taken care of." He hadn't planned to tell his father about the offer until he'd given it more thought, but it seemed appropriate to mention it now. He'd thought the old man would be more pleased.

"I see," he said. "And this is something you're considering?"

"I really just heard about it a little while ago," James said. "I've had a lot of other things on my mind."

"Hmm. Well. Could be good. Good solid institution. Not going out of business anytime soon."

"Why are you asking?"

He heard sounds coming from the other room, running footsteps and squeals, suggesting the kids had come downstairs and were getting ready for the program.

"Your mother and I were thinking maybe we could help you out, if you want our help. . . ."

"If you're talking about a loan, I don't—"

"I'm not. I'm talking about offering you financial security for the rest of your life, if you're willing to work for it. I know it's not the kind of work you've ever shown much interest in, but it's honest work. And it has its rewards, apart from the pecuniary, if you learn how to look at it."

When James realized what his father was about to offer him, he nearly fell out of his chair.

"I may not have always said so," the older man continued, "particularly after some of the stunts you pulled when you were younger, but I've always known you've got as good a head on your shoulders as any of my children. You and Julie were always the creative ones, so we let you go in your own directions and never pushed you toward the family business, but I've always known you could do anything you wanted if you set yourself to it. I know that banking isn't as glamorous as some of the things you may have in mind, but I asked a friend of mine over at the university and he told me there are numerous instances of men who were employed during the day and did their writing at night. He mentioned a man named Wallace Stevens, who was president of an insurance company in Hartford. And another fellow who was a doctor. I've forgotten his name. It was an odd name."

"William Carlos Williams?"

"That's it. And I recall from my college days that Melville was an accountant and Nathaniel Hawthorne was a customs inspector. So it can be done. There might be a long learning curve if you want to work at the bank, but you do get to the point where you leave your work at the office."

This was true. For the better part of James's childhood, his father had come home every night for dinner, usually reading the *Observer* or the *Wall Street Journal* and not talking to anybody, but always home.

"You want me to work in the bank?" James asked.

If James interpreted his father correctly, he wasn't talking about signing him on as a teller or loan officer. It seemed impossible to even consider that his father wanted James to take over the bank, now that Eric had turned him down and decided to stay in Denver, but what else could it mean? James felt sad, realizing how desperate his father had to be. The *Observer* frequently mentioned "century farms" that had been in the same family for more than a hundred years—Terry Kesler's, for one—and how losing such a farm was especially tragic and emotionally devastating because it meant the farmer felt like he was failing both his ancestors and his descendants. Terry had certainly gone off the deep end at the prospect. Onagle Federal Savings was a century bank, so to speak. James could only imagine the pressure his father was feeling at the thought of having no one in the family to take it over. He didn't know what to say, so he let his father keep talking.

"I just want you to think about it," his father said. "I don't want you to answer right now. I know it's not your idea of fun, but we don't always get to have jobs that are fun. I should think the majority of men dislike their jobs in some respects, but you make a sacrifice for your family and you find your happiness in other places. You can wish and dream otherwise, but I do believe I'm telling you the straight facts. A good job for life and a safe and attractive place to live is an offer many men would jump at, I should think.

"I don't want you to think we don't respect your dreams, because we do. We don't want to tell you not to be a writer, if that's what you want to do. We just wanted to increase your options, because it's my understanding that it's possible to do both. If you need to. If it would help things with Catherine. I do know that it's hard to start a family when things are unstable and insecure. So just think about it. And don't worry about not being up to it because I'd stay on for as long as it takes to get you up to speed and teach you everything I know. And I know you know there's a down side to the business, but you should also know that we help people every day. We help a lot of people every day. It's a business, not a charity, but ultimately it's a business that helps people. That's what my father told me, and I have come to understand that he was right.

"Well," he said. "That's my speech. I just wanted you to think about it. If it helps. We should join the others."

James was too stunned to respond.

Ten

THE PROGRAM BEGAN, AS IT DID EVERY YEAR, WITH the senior member of the family reading the Christmas story from the Bible, Luke 2, verses 1–14, beginning with, "And it came to pass in those days that a decree went out from Caesar Augustus that all the world should be registered . . ." and ending with, "Glory to God in the highest, and on earth peace, goodwill toward men!" James's father read the story in the same calm, solemn voice every year, as had his father and his father before

him, because they were Lutherans, who saw no need for inter-
pretive emphasis or overly dramatic renderings. The words
should speak for themselves.

Following the reading, the family sang a few carols, with Ruth
at the piano, accompanying the singing. They sang "Away in a
Manger," "O, Come, All Ye Faithful," and "*Jeg Er Så Glad Hver
Julekveld,*" and then it was time for the children, who announced
they had a skit prepared.

The skit began with five reindeer, including Rudolph, Donner,
Blitzen, Guido, and Lefty. Guido and Lefty wore black turtle-
necks pulled up to their noses, signifying that they were bad guys.
Rudolph wore a red stick-on foam-rubber clown's nose—Julie
had brought one for each of the kids.

In act one, Donner, Blitzen, Guido, and Lefty all made fun of
Rudolph and refused to let him play in any reindeer games—in this
case, hopscotch. In act two, true to the familiar song, Rudolph
guided Santa's sleigh through the fog using his shiny red nose as a
beacon, redeeming himself. In act three, however, there was a twist.
Donner and Blitzen accepted Rudolph and welcomed him to the
team, but Guido and Lefty continued to make fun of him, calling
him names like "Tomato Face" and "Pimple Snout" until he broke

down in tears. That night Guido and Lefty went so far as to deface Rudolph's house, portrayed by a large piece of construction paper, writing on it, "Rudolph Go Home" and "Red Noses Not Welcome." The next morning Donner and Blitzen came by, saw the graffiti, and tried to console Rudolph, who was once again reduced to tears.

In the final scene, Donner and Blitzen confronted Guido and Lefty, telling them they had no right to pick on other reindeer. Then Donner and Blitzen turned their backs to the audience and then turned around again to reveal that all the reindeer on Rudolph's team were wearing red foam-rubber noses in an act of reindeer solidarity. The skit ended with Rudolph, as played by Henry, making a brief plea for tolerance of others who might be different from everybody else, at which point Guido and Lefty donned red foam-rubber noses too. Then everybody sang "Rudolph, the Red-Nosed Reindeer."

By James's estimation, it was one of the best skits he'd ever seen, far better than anything he and his siblings had ever been able to cook up on such short notice. Abigail admitted the main idea had been Kirstin's.

The program concluded, as it always did, with the singing of "Silent Night," and then presents were distributed. James was pleased to see that his gifts were appreciated by his nieces and nephews, particularly when Thomas saw Paul's John Elway jersey and protested, "Hey, I wanted to be John Elway," only to open his own John Elway jersey a moment later.

No one mentioned Catherine. James was aware that some-one—Julie, probably, had culled from the pile beneath the tree any gifts addressed to Catherine or "to James and Catherine." He tried to push her from his thoughts, but at the same time, during the entire time that the presents were opened and indeed from the time dinner started, James had been listening for the telephone to ring. Maybe he was being silly, but after what they'd meant to each other, he couldn't believe Catherine wasn't going to call him on Christmas Eve. He could, of course, pick up the phone and call her, but he wanted her to be the one to feel the need.

When eleven o'clock came and it was time for everybody to put on their coats and head over to First Emmanuel for the candle-light service, he briefly considered swallowing his pride and call-ing her, but by then the differing time zones made it too late.

THE SIDEWALKS OUTSIDE THE CHURCH WERE LINED with luminarias, glowing ice globes made by filling ordinary balloons with water and letting them partially freeze. Once the outside was frozen, a hole was cracked in the top and the remaining liquid water poured out of center, after which the balloon was removed from the outside. What remained was a hollow sphere of clear ice that, James had to admit, looked pretty cool with a votive candle burning inside. His mother's friend Mrs. Jorganson, the current president of First Emmanuel's Ladies Activities Circle, had come across the idea in an old *Reader's Digest*. A semicircle of luminarias lit the crèche like footlights on an ancient stage, the holy figurines still wearing shrouds of snow from yesterday's blizzard.

The Englers sat in the same pews every Sunday, and every Christmas Eve, three quarters of the way toward the front on the right side of the right-hand aisle. The family had, in fact, sat in the same pews since the turn of the century. (The Larsons sat three quarters of the way toward the front of the nave on the left side of the left-hand aisle.) James sat between his sister Julie and his nephew Henry, who'd been allowed to bring along a Winnie the Pooh coloring book.

As an adolescent, the last time he'd been a regular churchgoer, James had scorned the dabblers who only attended services once a year, on Christmas Eve, but now that he'd become one of them, he had more sympathy. He sang the carols, taking the red hymnal from the rack on the back of the pew in front of him and doing his best to sight-read the bass parts. He listened to a choir member sing "O Holy Night" in a lush baritone and remembered how that song had once given him goose bumps. As he listened to Pastor Gruening's sermon about humble beginnings, great surprises, and the promise of God's love, James recalled how he'd had a hard time, after Gerry's death, understanding how a benevolent God could hear a nine-year-old boy utter the words "I hope you never come back" to his older brother and then grant that boy his wish.

He still had a hard time with it.

That question always led to the larger question of evil, for which James had never found a satisfactory answer. And that led, with equal inevitability, to the irreconcilable inconsistencies of believers who credited God with miracles when something good happened, unshakably convinced in the knowledge and certain proof of divine intervention, but who shrugged their shoulders and said, "We don't know. It's just one of those mysteries," when something horrible happened—when a baby stopped breathing in her crib or a madman with an automatic weapon opened fire in a crowd. James didn't understand how the apparent inability to explain the latter didn't deter such believers from explaining the former. Nor did he care for the way the doctrinal options were traditionally freighted, presented as a choice between believing and going to heaven or not believing and going to hell. The choice seemed a tad bullying, which was one reason he'd stopped going to church.

The conclusion he'd always reached was simply (but it was hardly simple) to let the unknowable remain unknown and live with the ambiguities. In the end, either way, you still had to live your life by being as moral a person as you could be, regardless of what specific belief system you endorsed. What he'd always believed in, when he couldn't believe in anything else, was love.

He looked around the church, wondering how many other people in the room were currently reviewing their doubts. For him, at least, church always seemed to raise more questions than it answered. Maybe that was how it was supposed to be. At any rate, it would certainly be easier to believe in love if he went home to find a message from Catherine on his parents' answering machine. She, after all, had been the one who questioned his belief in love. "I know you believe in love, but sometimes I'm not even sure if you *like* being in love. It's supposed to make you feel good, not nervous."

She had a point.

In the pew in front of him, Eric sat with his arms around his sons. Paul and Thomas both appeared restless, no doubt anxious to get home and play with their new toys. Studying his brother's toupee closely, he decided it looked truly natural and real. He observed Lisa with her perfect posture, her girls sitting equally straight beside her, their hair tied back with matching ribbons. Looking at his siblings with their families, James couldn't help wondering if he'd ever have one of his own.

"You can go to the bathroom after the service," Eric was whispering to Thomas.

"But I have to go *now*," Thomas complained, loudly enough to make Mrs. Jorganson, in a nearby pew, smile.

"Five more minutes and we'll go," Eric said.

James considered what his father had said to him. The offer had seemed preposterous. It certainly wasn't going to get Catherine back, nor was it an offer he could have brought to her even in their best days. She'd spoken fondly enough of her visits to Onagle and the feeling she got there, the sense of community and the slower pace. A visit was one thing, but moving there permanently was quite another. Catherine was a city girl through and through. That much would never change.

Now, after giving it more thought, James still found the offer preposterous, but he could see how his father might be thinking, trying to do him a favor and at the same time trying to hang on to what was most valuable to him. When James asked himself if he could work in banking, study hard, apply himself, learn the ropes, and try with all his might to persevere, he thought maybe he could. Maybe. Maybe his father's faith in him was not entirely misplaced, or maybe running a bank wasn't as hard as it looked. It probably was as hard as it looked, actually, though he believed he could do it if he had to. Yet when he asked himself if working at the bank was the reason he was placed on earth or the best way to utilize his talents, the answer was a resounding no.

The choir began singing "Silent Night" as the lights in the church dimmed. The ushers went down the aisles with lit tapers and helped everyone light the candles they'd been handed along with their bulletins. One candle lit another until the church glowed to the light of hundreds of small flames. There was a long moment of silence after the hymn ended. Faces smiled at each other in the candlelight. Then the lights came up to close the service, the music swelling into a rousing organ arrangement of "Joy to the World!"

Worshipers stood and began moving into the aisles and milling about, exchanging Christmas greetings and chatting amiably. James shook hands and spoke with many of his parents' oldest friends, people he now saw only in encounters like these during the holidays. With his engagement party canceled, he knew people were talking. Some seemed to gaze on him with looks of sympathy or perhaps pity, but that couldn't be helped. A canceled engagement would hardly cause so much as a raised eyebrow in New York City, but in a small town like Onagle, it was a big deal.

He watched his father and Eugene Larson pretending not to notice each other, though at one point they were a mere ten feet apart. His mother was less subtle about it, heading for the ladies' room just as Joyce Larson appeared to be looking for her.

James was standing in the front hall adjoining the narthex when he spotted Sarah talking to Ben Larson. Sarah was wearing a black sweater, a tan skirt, and knee-high black boots. Ben wore a sweater vest and a bow tie. He'd begun to turn gray at the temples but still looked fit. The last James had heard, Ben was a commodities trader in Chicago.

As much as James felt like avoiding Ben Larson out of family solidarity, another part of him felt—what? Jealous? Not, of course, in any romantic sense. Nevertheless, his pulse quickened to see Ben talking to Sarah, an ancient rivalry still operating like some kind of phantom ache.

He crossed over to say hello.

"Hey, J.B.," Sarah said. "Merry Christmas. How you guys doing?"

"Merry, merry," he replied. "Hey, Ben. What's new? Still swapping pork bellies at the Merc?"

"Actually, I'm in the corn pit," Ben said. "You're still back east?"

"He's a New Yorker," Sarah told Ben. "His whole life is like the opening credits of *Saturday Night Live*. He even saw Madonna once in a disco."

"Did you?"

"Well, it was a guy, but he looked just like Madonna," James said. "So how was the party?"

"Festive. My mother made a giant punch bowl of eggnog from scratch and then poured it down the sink at the last minute when she freaked out at the idea of serving her friends three dozen raw eggs. Other than that, same old, same old. We missed seeing your folks, though given all the stuff going on around here, it was probably just as well."

Ben was the only person in the world whom James had ever struck in anger, albeit in the middle of a pickup hockey game at the park one February night, when players punching each other in anger was not uncommon. Mike had stepped between them to prevent further hostilities.

"What do you mean by that, Ben?" James asked, trying to keep the emotion from his voice. Could the guy truly be unaware of how much it had hurt James's parents not to be invited to the party? "What 'stuff' are you talking about?"

"Calm down, Jim," Ben replied. "I'm just saying your folks were missed and it was too bad, okay? But given what's been happening, between the banking crisis and the farm crisis and all, it just hasn't been entirely comfortable lately when bankers and farmers get in the same room. Nobody's blaming anybody. We're all just doing our jobs, but that's the way it is.

And my dad doesn't care, but to some people, it matters. I didn't think you'd been gone so long that that would be lost on you."

"It's not lost on me, Ben," James said, trying not to raise his voice. "What is lost on me is how, after all these years, you still don't know my family." He wanted to say so much more, until he remembered where he was and what night it was. Ben looked a little shocked at being confronted.

"See you Tuesday night," Ben said to Sarah at last. He glanced at James before turning.

James watched him go.

"Nice going, Otis," Sarah said.

"Was I just a colossal idiot?" James asked her.

"Pretty much," she said. "So was he, but he was born that way. What's your excuse?"

"I've been under a lot of stress," he told her. He realized how much anger he was carrying around inside of him, anger that had nothing to do with Ben Larson—or with the news about Mike, for that matter. "Think Santa heard that?"

"Well, he knows when you've been bad or good," she said. "There's no getting around that."

"I think I blew it."

"Leave some extra cookies," she suggested.

"He's coming Tuesday?"

"He's coming tonight," Sarah said. "He lands on your roof with his reindeer and sleigh. Surely someone told you."

"Not Santa. Ben."

"It looks like a lot of people are going to be there," she said. "I can't help it. I still feel sorry for him. He's a nice guy, deep down, but he thinks people don't like him, so he acts unlikable, and then people *really* don't like him."

"He's kind of a mystery that way," James agreed.

"You having a tough night?" she asked.

"I keep thinking she should have called. Regardless of whatever else, she should have called. It's Christmas Eve."

"You're right. She should have."

"She should have, right? That's not unreasonable to expect, is it?"

"Maybe there'll be a message waiting for you when you get home."

"Maybe," he said. "I've got this stupid idea that if she

doesn't call, it means it's really over. Even though I already know it's really over. But this is like the last nail in the coffin or something."

She stepped closer to him, put her arms around him, and hugged him close, resting her head against his chest—the kind of hug that said the hugger needed it as much as the hugged. She squeezed his arms.

"J.B., you've been a nice guy since you were five," she said, looking him in the eye. "You were a problem before that, but from then on, you were fine. Nice guys do okay. It's just a myth about finishing last. You'll get through this."

She straightened. "I should go find Martha. She's my ride. Call me later if you need to."

"I will," he said. "If I do."

He went to look for his parents. Julie asked James who the babe he was talking to was. He said he didn't know what "babe" Julie was talking about.

"The girl," Julie said, "in the tan skirt and boots."

"Who?" he said. "Sarah? That wasn't a babe. That was Sarah Brown."

"*That* was little Sarah Brown?"

"Yeah."

"She's changed," Julie said.

ON THEIR WAY HOME THEY PASSED MIKE'S CHURCH, St. Mary's, where the midnight mass was still going on. He remembered something Mike had said once: "Don't you wish you could meet a girl who was like Sarah, except more girly?"

James realized Sarah really had changed. She was still Sarah, but she was different too.

Definitely more girly.

And that, suddenly, was rather interesting.

Eleven

IT TOOK NEARLY HALF AN HOUR TO PUT THE KIDS
to bed, the big house filling with the plaintive wails and beseeching moans of children hoping to get five more minutes with their
new toys. Once the house quieted, a few rituals remained to be
performed. There were stockings to be filled by "Santa Claus,"
who came during the night, affording a second opening of presents Christmas morning, though only for the kids.

Lisa and Rachel busied themselves in the den. Eric was at the dining room table, trying to figure out how to wrap the guitars he'd bought for Paul and Thomas. Julie was in the kitchen drying the dishes as Joe washed, singing "O Little Town of Bethlehem" softly under his breath as he worked. Behind them, James's mother prepared the dough for the cinnamon rolls she'd bake fresh in the morning.

James felt his pulse quicken when he noticed that the red light on the answering machine was blinking. He considered ignoring it, going straight to bed and dealing with it in the morning, but the compulsion to know was too strong. There were two messages.

Neither was from Catherine.

He put down the phone, unexpectedly devastated. Perhaps he'd inherited, more than he knew, his father's need for connection during the holidays. Perhaps he still cared about Catherine more than he liked to admit. Either way, he'd held out hope, picturing a Christmas Eve phone call in which Catherine would tell him she missed him and he'd say he missed her and she'd say, "This is crazy. What are we doing? Let's give it one more try." He'd even pictured, years from now, telling her the phone call was the best Christmas present he'd ever gotten.

"Honey," his mother said. "Would you mind going out and bringing in another load of wood? Not the birch. The oak. Do you know which is which?"

"I haven't lived in the city *that* long," he told her. .

He welcomed the diversion. The sky was overcast and starless, the floodlight on the barn like a light ship floating in a dark sea.

He'd filled the canvas tote with a dozen pieces of seasoned oak and was returning to the house when he noticed Cully was still up, the cottage window lit blue by the light of the television inside. His first thought was that something was wrong. Cully usually spent Christmas in St. Paul with his sister. Even though he customarily kept to himself, if they'd known he had stayed home, they would have asked him to join them.

When James went to check to make sure everything was all right, he looked in the window and saw the old handyman asleep in his recliner, a folding tray next to him with some book opened face down on it. He had a crossword puzzle open on his lap, the pencil fallen from his hand. A black-and-white movie was showing on the television—something featuring Katharine Hepburn and Spencer Tracy, though James couldn't identify it. Cully wore pajamas and an old plaid bathrobe frayed at the cuffs and collar, a pair of felt Sorel boot liners on his feet for slippers. There was a cup of tea on the tray with the tea bag still in it. A dented stainless-steel teakettle with a cracked handle rested on the wood stove. There were no Christmas decorations that James could see, save for a single Christmas card propped open and upright on the kitchen table.

The image was one of aching loneliness. It was, in that sense, terrifying.

He used the phone in the den, though it was past midnight Iowa time, and dialed the New York number, not knowing what he was going to say but willing to ask Catherine to reconsider one last time. Maybe he'd even mention the offer his father had made, see how it played. . . .

After four rings, her parents' answering machine picked up.

"We're not home right now, so please leave a message," Catherine's father's recorded voice said. "You know what to do."

If only he did. He hung up without leaving a message.

LYING IN HIS CHILDHOOD BED, HE FELT ANOTHER dark moment coming on. Everybody had them, didn't they?

This was just one of those long dark nights of the soul when hope seems lost—which was, he allowed, why the eastern star in the nativity story shines as such a powerful image in the human imagination, a symbol of hope and promise. James looked out his bedroom window. It was the same window he'd looked out as a child, hoping to spot Santa's sleigh arriving from the North Pole. Later he'd looked for jet planes, fantasizing that his brother was still up there, looking for a place to land but somehow unable to come down because everybody had forgotten about him. Tonight he saw neither stars nor sleighs nor jet planes, just a black expanse above a winter landscape.

He tried to sleep but couldn't. At first he was just overwhelmingly sad, unable to picture the future, but then he felt a bleak emptiness filling him that was much worse than sad, because sadness is a feeling you know is wrong. The emptiness seemed somehow to bring with it a sense of appropriateness. He was growing less frightened by it.

He got up around three and tiptoed to the bathroom. He considered calling Catherine again, though he knew he couldn't. At the top of the landing, he noticed a light on downstairs. He went down to turn it off and realized somebody had left the

Christmas tree plugged in. Worrying that it might present a fire hazard, he went to unplug the tree. Then he saw his father sitting on the sofa.

"Hey," he said, surprised. "What are you doing up?"

"Had to take my medication," his father said. "Then I thought I'd come down here for a minute."

"Is everything okay?" James asked. "What medication are you on?"

"Nothing serious. Just a blood thinner."

"I'm sorry to hear that."

"Your dad's an old man, Jimmy."

"You can still haul more wood than I can," James said. There was a pause. "I don't think I can accept your offer. I'm sorry."

"Of course you can't," his father said, nodding. "I think I knew that before I brought it up."

"I'm really flattered, though. I can't even tell you."

"Not a good time to go into banking anyway," his father said. "It's not just the little S&Ls that are having a hard time."

James heard a weariness in his father's voice he hadn't noticed before, and it wasn't from the late hour. For the first time, he realized that his father longed to step back from his work and retire.

He was the most responsible man James had ever known. During his teen years, when he had been defiant and unruly and his father had called him irresponsible, his thought had been, *Compared to you, I probably am, but compared to other kids my age, you don't know what you're talking about.* For all their battles, he'd always known his father was a good man. He'd known how important it was to him to be honest and truthful, to have integrity and dignity and to live a moral life. He couldn't imagine the weight his father must have been carrying on his shoulders, with so many of the local farmers and business people, friends he'd known for years, holding him responsible for their own failures.

Walter Engler IV was frugal, but he was not venal or avaricious. That wasn't how he was built. James understood how much it hurt his father not to be invited to the Larsons' party. The need to belong is not a need that goes away with time or fades with age.

"Have you talked to Joe about the bank?" James said. "He'd be a natural."

"No, not yet," Walter said. "We wanted to talk to you first. We do understand, you know."

A log snapped in the fireplace, shooting an ember from the dying flames that bounced off the chain-link fire screen.

"I know, Dad. And I appreciate it. But the problems Cath and I are having aren't the kind that are going to fix themselves by relocating the problem. Your point about stability and security is well taken, but that wasn't it. The problem was communication. Or the absence of it. And that's as much my fault as hers. That and a general lack of faith."

"What was it she lacked faith in?" his father asked. James had been thinking about this.

"Not her," he admitted. "Me. I couldn't . . . I don't know. There was always something . . . holding me back, I guess."

"I see."

"It means a lot to me that you thought I could work at the bank."

"We've always had faith in you, James. Do you know your mother's saved every letter you wrote home from Mill River? We always knew you were a beautiful writer. She didn't want to send you, you know. She wanted to keep you here with us.

And I know you wanted to stay. I'm sorry if we did the wrong thing."

"It was the right decision," James said. "I was just a bit resistant to change at the time. I didn't think I'd make any friends. Speaking of which, did you hear they're having Mike Quinn's party without him, after the memorial service?"

"Your mother told me. Would you like to ride over with us?"

"You're going?"

"To the service. Unless you'd rather go alone."

"No, no," James said. "Let's go together."

The two men stared at the tree, the soft white lights reflecting a thousandfold in the mirrored ornaments. They listened to the fire in the hearth, hissing as it burned. James looked over and noticed that his father held a glass of water in his hands. When the old man took a sip, James saw that his father appeared to be on the verge of weeping, tears pooling up in the corners of his eyes, and that he'd taken Gerry's picture down from the mantle and set it on the table at the end of the couch.

James looked at the picture of his brother in uniform. Gerry had been a good-looking guy, with a bright smile. He'd also been the one male authority figure in the family James had found emotionally accessible, more like a friend he could talk to, a guy who wasn't always on his side but who always told him the straight story. James was now older than Gerry had been at the time of his death, which meant Gerry was becoming the baby in the family.

"How often do you think about him?" James said.

"Oh, every day," his father said. "Every day. Every hour, really. You never stop loving your children, you know. You can't. It's not humanly possible."

James somehow hadn't realized. He'd assumed his father had locked the memory away somewhere, steeling himself behind some stoical resolve not to grieve. How ridiculous. Of course he hadn't.

"The last thing I said to him was, 'I hope you never come back.' Did you know that? When his plane crashed, I thought I caused it. I was worried that his last thought was that he was mad at me. I thought you'd be mad at me too. I couldn't even look at you."

How many years had he longed to tell his father about those last words?

"I'm sorry you thought that," his father said. "That must have really bothered you."

"It did. A lot."

"You ever talk to anybody about it?"

"I couldn't. Not at first. Then I talked to Mike about it, the day he told me he was joining the air force, and I told him, if he died, I wasn't coming to his funeral. I seem to have a facility for saying the wrong things to people."

"What did Mike say?"

"He said I was being melodramatic. And that if you could make something happen by wishing it, everybody would be as good-looking as he was."

"What did Gerry say when you said you wished he'd never come back?"

"He said, 'Don't sweat it, Squirt.'"

"Well, that sounds like good advice to me," Walter said.

James looked at the photograph in the picture frame. When he remembered his older brother, he remembered a guy who always had time to play with him when everybody else in the family was busy. He remembered a baby-sitter who let him stay up as late as he wanted on the condition that when their parents came home, James would jump into bed and pretend he'd been asleep for hours. He remembered playing catch after supper during the long summer evenings, his shadow longer than he could toss the ball, Gerry teaching him how to bat and pitch and throwing the ball to him harder than anybody ever had, explaining that if he could learn to catch the hard ones, the balls that got hit to him in games would seem easy.

He suddenly remembered what their last fight had been about. He'd asked his brother to play catch with him, but Gerry had begged off, saying he was running late and besides, there were six inches of snow on the ground.

"When he'd come home in his uniform," James said, "I remember being impressed and proud of him, but I couldn't wait until he changed into his regular clothes again. And then, when his leave was over and he'd come down in his uniform again, carrying his bags, I couldn't stand it. I was so scared for him. But I couldn't tell him that. I knew he had to go, but I couldn't understand why."

"I know," the old man said. "I know you were scared."

He took his father's hand and squeezed it. His father had always had strong, meaty hands. James couldn't remember the last time he'd held his father's hand, but it felt different. It was thinner. The skin was looser. He squeezed and his father squeezed back, and then they let go of each other when they heard Ruth coming down the stairs. She was in her bathrobe.

"What are my boys doing up so late?" she asked.

"Just waiting for Santa Claus," James said.

"Can I fix you a sandwich?" she asked James.

"No, thanks," he said, smiling to think there was no time, day or night, when his mother didn't think it appropriate to try to feed him. "I don't think I'm going to need to eat for a week."

"Maybe a piece of *lefse*?" she asked.

"Well, maybe one," he said.

She brought out a small plate, and they all had a snack. "I think I'll go to bed," his father said finally.

"I think I'll sit awhile longer," James said.

He threw two more pieces of oak on the fire, good hard wood that would burn a long time. The embers soon came to life. He sat down on the couch, listening to the fire crackle. He watched the flames for a while, pondering, then closed his eyes.

HE AWOKE TO THE SOUNDS OF KIRSTIN, ABIGAIL, Paul, Thomas, and Henry whispering and giggling. Somebody had covered him during the night with a chenille throw. Lisa,

Joe, Eric, and Rachel were at the dining room table, eating cinnamon rolls and sipping coffee. His mother brought him a cup, so he sat up and watched his nieces and nephews open the presents Santa had brought them. Paul and Thomas immediately struck rock-and-roll poses with their new guitars, grimacing like the soulful bluesmen they hoped to be one day. It was sweet how the older kids, who knew Santa wasn't real, refused to spoil it for the younger ones who still believed in him.

As he watched them, James recalled the last gift he'd bought for Gerry, shoveling sidewalks and driveways until he'd earned enough money to buy his big brother a new Wilson baseball mitt with Roberto Clemente's name written across the palm as if he'd signed it himself.

After all the presents were opened, James said he had an announcement to make.

"This is for any nieces, nephews, or grown-ups who might be interested. I will be leading a sledding expedition, in approximately one hour, to a place called Dead Man's Hill." The children looked appropriately awed by the title. "So dress warmly and come prepared. The toboggans are in the barn. Resume playing with amusing objects."

JAMES WAS LEANING AGAINST THE FIREPLACE MANTEL, talking to Joe, when he saw an envelope stuck behind the firewood box at the end of the hearth.

"I don't know if you heard," Joe was saying, with a subdued excitement in his voice, "but Walter asked me this morning if I wanted to come work for him at the bank and stay on after he retires. It looks like Lisa and the girls and I might be moving down to Onagle."

"I think that's terrific," James said as he retrieved up the stray envelope, thinking to add it to the fire, until he noticed it hadn't been opened. Joe had grown up in a small town. He'd like Onagle. Lisa wouldn't care where she lived, as long as she had her gardens and her family. It might take the girls a while, but eventually they'd adjust.

"I think it's a great opportunity for you," James said, still looking at the envelope he held in his hand. At first he thought it was a Christmas card that had somehow fallen behind the box while the others were being opened and displayed. When he saw the return address, he handed the envelope to his mother, who slit the side of the envelope with a letter opener and shook out the invitation to the Larson's party.

Twelve

REACHING THE FOURTEENTH FAIRWAY AND DEAD
Man's Hill required a challenging trek through the woods. Lisa
and Joe had brought their cross-country skis down from the
Twin Cities, and there were enough banged-up spare pairs in the
basement to equip a regiment of Norwegian resistance fighters.
Two toboggans were deployed, a three-person model and a six-
person toboggan that James's father and uncles had sledded on
when they were boys.

The hill, which had seemed so daunting to James as a child, didn't look all that scary anymore.

"Can you believe how terrified we used to be of this place?" he asked Julie.

"I think that was Gerry making us think it was more danger-ous than it was," she said. They watched the kids as they sledded. Thomas was the biggest daredevil, but Kirstin was right there with him, hanging on as their toboggan went airborne. Henry stood at the top of the hill, holding his mother's hand and observing as he worked up his nerve.

"So how long are you staying around?" Julie asked.

"I don't know," James said. "I'm not in any rush to get back."

"If you want company for New Year's Eve, you can stay with me in Chicago before you go back," Julie said. "I know Chicago isn't as cool as New York, but my friends are having a party. I could introduce you to my friend Jen—"

"Don't even start," he told her. "Besides, New York is really special on New Year's Eve. I love waking up New Year's morn-ing and going skating on the puddles of frozen urine left behind by the drunks in Times Square. Did I tell you the city took away the port-a-potties last year because they thought it would discourage people from drinking too much? And none of the bars or restaurants in Times Square will let anybody use their bathrooms."

"Lovely," she said. "This is information I didn't need to know."

"I talked to Dad last night," he said. "I got up and saw the lights on downstairs. Three in the morning. He was sitting on the couch, and he'd taken Gerry's picture from the mantel."

"What'd you talk about?" she asked.

"Lots of things," he said. "Mostly Gerry."

"What about Gerry?"

"Just what we remembered. I think Dad had been crying."

"Really?"

"Little bit," James said. "It's the holidays."

"It's more than that," Julie said.

CHRISTMAS DAY PASSED UNEVENTFULLY. IN THE AFTER-noon James watched a Lakers-Celtics game with his nephews.

"I think Magic Johnson is the best player ever," Paul said.

"Larry Bird is better," Thomas said.

"Nuh-uh," Paul said.

"Yuh-huh," Thomas said. "He's sneakier."

"Kevin McHale is funny looking," Henry opined.

"In what way?" James asked.

"He has funny arms."

"You're right," James said. "He does have funny arms."

He remembered playing half-court basketball games with Mike Quinn and how irritating it had been to try to defend against the larger boy. Mike was one of those players who'd perfected the art of dribbling in backward with his large rear end in your face, bulling his way until he was under the basket, then turning and shooting. On the other hand, James always liked having Mike on his side against other kids at the playground, working the give-and-go with him almost as if they knew what they were doing.

Lisa and Joe loaded up their minivan after dinner and headed home with the girls, followed by Eric and Rachel and the boys in their rented car, to spend a few days together in the Twin Cities. Henry said good-bye by sticking his parrot out the window. The bird said, "Merry Christmas, Uncle Jim! See you next year—aawk!" as they drove away. That evening James played a game of Scrabble with his mother and Julie while his father read his World War I book by the fireplace. Julie won the Scrabble game by three points. Nobody talked about Mike or mentioned Catherine, which was fine by James.

He went to bed early and read himself to sleep, taking from the shelf one of the James Bond books he'd read as an adolescent. He remembered playing spies with Mike well into the seventh grade, an unspoken secret pact between them, since they both knew they were too old to be playing spies anymore.

When he awoke, he had breakfast with Julie and then helped her carry her bags to her Jeep. Before she left, she gave him a big hug.

"I'll be thinking of you, little brother," she said. "You could still come see me in Chicago on your way home."

"Maybe I will," he said. "I've always wanted to go to the Art Institute. Do they still have Hopper's *Nighthawks*?"

"And *American Gothic*. And *Dempsey and Firpo's* there on loan— all in the same room," she said. "It's like the grand slam of American paintings."

"Wouldn't there have to be four to make it a grand slam?" he said.

"I'm working on it," she said. "I love you, little brother."

"I love you, big sister," he said.

"Well?" she said.

"Well, what?"

"Where's the parting shot? Aren't you going to say something insulting about my weight?"

"Not today," he said. "Don't really feel like it."

"Now I *am* worried," she said. She hugged him again and kissed him on the cheek. "Be good," she said. "Call me if you need to talk."

"Are you still at the same number?" he asked. He added, "Or did they give your butt its own area code?"

"That's better," she said, getting into her Jeep. "And by the way, your friend Sarah, the one you were talking to at church?"

"What about her?"

"Just pay attention. That's all I'm going to say."

AT THE MEMORIAL SERVICE THAT AFTERNOON, JAMES saw a number of childhood friends, kids he'd known from grade school, from Boy Scouts, from summer sports teams, and from hanging out at the lake or the bowling alley. It took him a while to recognize many of them. His friend Mitch had lost all his hair. Adam was barely recognizable behind his beard. Sally had turned prematurely gray and wore glasses. Kyle appeared to have gained at least a hundred pounds. Schultz was exactly the same.

James felt guilty at how far he'd fallen out of touch. He didn't really belong here anymore, didn't know what was going on in town, didn't know the small things that might be covered by gossip or the larger things the *Observer* was talking about—the school-bond issue or the problems out at the water treatment plant. Yet he didn't feel like a New Yorker either. He wondered where he did belong, and if the problem was more internal than external. There were probably people who felt like they fit in wherever they went. Perhaps it was simply an emotional faculty, one he lacked. Some people were extroverted. Some people were shy. Some people felt like they didn't belong, and he was one of them. He wished he wasn't, but what could he do?

He felt a tug on his sleeve. Sarah was wearing a black skirt and a royal blue sweater, her black knee-high boots giving her an extra two inches of height.

"Hey, J.B.," she said, giving James a hug and a pat on the back. He returned the hug. "How you doing?"

"Okay," he said, sniffling. He realized he'd probably caught her cold, but there was something about that he liked. "How about you?" Her cold sounded, if anything, worse, or perhaps she'd been crying.

"Been better," she said. "Did she call?" He shook his head. "I'm sorry, J.B."

"She didn't call, but I got the message," he said. "I'm glad you're here."

"See anybody you know?" she asked him.

"I see people I know I *should* know," he told her. It seemed like the whole town had turned out to remember Mike. Sarah pointed out an older woman standing alone near the water cooler.

"There's a familiar face," Sarah said.

James recognized their fourth-grade teacher, Mrs. Mooney, by her erect posture and by the fur coat she wore, a modest garment of dark mink that he remembered her wearing when he was young—a gift from her late husband, she'd told the class when she'd used the coat to introduce a lesson on the French-Canadian fur trappers who'd opened up the interior of the New World. She looked the same, perhaps a bit grayer, her long neck slightly more wattled with time, now graced by a strand of pearls. She'd probably only been in her forties when James was her pupil, but back then all adults had seemed ancient to him. For some reason, James couldn't remember ever seeing her outside of school.

James and Sarah made their way over to her.

"Mrs. Mooney?" Sarah said. "Hi. I don't know if you remember me, but—"

"Sarah Brown," the teacher said. "Of course I remember you. You sound like you've got that bug that's been going around. And Mr. Engler. How've you been?" Her voice was still raspy, and there was something about the way she maintained a direct, unblinking eye contact that reminded him why he'd always found her a bit menacing. Now, of course, he was at least a foot taller than she was. Back then she'd loomed over his desk and seemed all-knowing and powerful. "And where are you living now?"

"Manhattan," he said. "I'm actually in graduate school and working as a teaching assistant."

"And whom do you assist?" she asked.

"Well, nobody, but that's what they call us," he said. He felt foolish, trying to talk to her teacher-to-teacher. She was clearly the master. "Actually, I've been offered a teaching position at my old school."

"Well, good for you," she said. "I know you were one of Michael's closest friends. I hope you're not offended if I say this, but even though I remember all my students, he was truly one of the special ones. He truly was. Not necessarily a star pupil, but a star individual. He was the sort of child teachers look forward to seeing every day. Not that I didn't love you all."

"I know what you mean," James said.

"Are you going to take it?" she asked. He wasn't sure what she meant. "The teaching position you said you've been offered?"

"I'm still mulling it over," he said.

"Will you let me know what you decide?" she asked him. He was surprised to think she could be interested.

"Sure," he said.

"Will you be coming to the Supper Club afterwards?" Sarah asked.

"I don't think I can," Mrs. Mooney said. "I'm flying out to San Diego in the morning to see my sister, and I haven't begun to pack. You know how long it takes us old people to get ready for trips. But you'll tell everyone they're in my thoughts and prayers, won't you? It's good to see you again."

James saw Terry and Martha in the coatroom, where Terry was helping Martha off with her coat. Terry looked surprisingly respectable in his dark suit, but then James had only seen him in sweatshirts and feed caps.

"I told Martha I'd sit with them," Sarah told James. "See you afterward."

James sat with his parents three-quarters of the way down the nave on the right-hand side. Across the chapel he saw Ben Larson, sitting alone.

He looked around. He hadn't spent much time in Catholic churches and was unfamiliar with some of the architectural features. He recognized the stations of the cross carved into the chapel walls, but he was uncertain of their liturgical function. Perhaps a third of the service was unfamiliar to him as well, the priest, Father Costello, beseeching, "Holy Mother of God, pray for us now," which was not the sort of thing one might hear in a Lutheran church, but the words about the promise of resurrection and eternal life ("And on the third day, he rose again. . . .") were the same. James remembered them from his brother's funeral. He remembered how angry he'd been, how the voice in his head kept saying, *It's not true, it's not true. They're just saying that because they want it to be true.* He recalled how much he wanted to run out of the church, go to the playground, find some pals to play with—anything but sit there and listen to what the minister was saying.

After a hymn, Mike's sister Rosemary, the oldest child in the family, addressed the assembly. He remembered her as tall and a little scary. Now he saw that she really was tall—nearly six feet—but not particularly scary in her gray suit and pulled-back, graying hair. James noticed an American flag pin fastened to her collar. The other members of Mike's family wore similar pins.

Rosemary began by thanking everyone for coming, then apologized as she pulled out a loose sheaf of papers. "I'm not much of a public speaker," she said, "so if you'll all bear with me, I'd like to read a few thoughts that I wrote down."

A pair of reading glasses hung from a chain around her neck. She put them on. She took a deep breath and looked out at the audience one last time, glancing over the top of her glasses as she adjusted the microphone.

"First of all, I want to tell you that my brother Michael loved being an American. He loved serving his country and he loved the men he served it with, and more than anything, he loved flying helicopters. He told me, 'Rosie, I can't believe I get paid to do this. I'd pay to do it if they weren't paying me.'

"But you know, in a way, Mikey was flying from the day he was born. I remember how happy I was on the day he was born to have my own living doll to play with, and a living doll he remained. He was, hands down, the most cheerful baby I've ever seen, and as a fully employed baby-sitter for most of my adolescence, I'd seen my share of fussy babies. Michael was just the opposite. I remember one time when my parents left me in charge and Michael was sick and throwing up in his crib, but even though he was sick, he was smiling and clapping his hands.

"The thing you could say about Michael was that he loved people. He *loved* people. When he was a toddler, we had problems taking him to restaurants because he never stayed in his seat—he wanted to go table to table and visit people and ask them what they were eating. We had a similar problem in the neighborhood where we lived, because Michael liked to let himself into other people's houses. Sometimes he'd do it when the neighbors weren't home, but it was actually worse when they were. Our neighbor Mrs. Jenkins was a sweet, elderly woman, and she was quite surprised one day when she was taking a bath and Michael wandered into her bathroom and asked her what she was doing.

"As he grew up, Michael became proficient at fixing anything that moved, from skateboards to go-carts. We had an old lawn mower engine that I think he used in about five or six different vehicles of his own design. Seven, I suppose, if you count the lawn mower. He had an extraordinary faith that there wasn't anything he could take apart that he couldn't put back together again. It was a faith in himself, but it was also a faith in the way things were, a belief that there was a logic to the universe and that if you just kept trying long enough and didn't lose your cool, you could get a handle on just about anything."

James listened to the words and thought of his old friend, sad that his life had ended too soon but satisfied that he'd lived it in the right way. His image of Mike as someone who was naïve or uncomplicated was wrong. He was as complicated as anybody else. He was just happier.

James's thoughts drifted. He wondered what people would say about him at his funeral. He couldn't imagine. That he was usually on time? That he made his bed in the morning? That he generally knew how to mind his own business? That he tried hard to love, even though he never quite got the hang of it? A balanced and fair assessment would have to list the negatives with the positives. He wasted time. He ultimately disappointed the people who loved him. He made his fiancée cry until she had to leave. He didn't live up to his potential.

He told himself he really needed to change things, but in a voice that sounded smaller than the last time he'd heard it. Perhaps one of the functions of a funeral was to send everyone home vowing to live better lives. Sometimes he felt more inclined, he had to admit, to quit trying and give up—those times when that black, empty, hollow feeling was overwhelming, and he felt so tired, and all he wanted to do was surrender to the feeling and let it wash over him until it washed him away.

He came back to Rosemary's words.

"For those of you who might have thought of Michael as fearless, I can assure you that that wasn't true. He was like anybody else, but I suppose if I had to say the one thing he was most afraid of, I'd say it was loneliness. Everybody here knows how friendly and outgoing Michael was, but there was something beyond friendliness driving it. I asked him once recently if he wanted to get married, and he told me he wanted to, but he said, 'Rosie, I've just seen too many military wives go through too much to put someone I love through that. The worst thing I can think of is being alone. I guess when I meet the woman who makes me want to give up the air force, I'll know I've met the right person.'"

For the first time in her eulogy, her voice broke, sending a wave of emotion rippling through the church.

"He never met her, but I know he was looking. He was afraid of loneliness, and that's probably one of the reasons why he had so many friends," she continued. "He had friends here in town, and he had friends in the air force, to be sure, and if they weren't all on duty in the Persian Gulf, I think you'd be amazed at how many would have been here today.

"Some of you are probably aware that when a serviceman dies in the line of duty, it's the commanding officer's responsibility to write a letter to the family. Well, they tell me this has never happened before, but I want you to know that after the air force notification team drove out to break the news to us in person, they brought letters not only from Michael's superior officer, Colonel Cruz, but from nearly every man in Michael's unit—

over two hundred of them, each one telling us a story of some kindness Michael had done, sometimes without even telling the recipient he'd done it. They were all so wonderful. I'm not sure how we'll ever be able to thank everyone."

She took a sip from a glass of water.

"But I think if Michael is looking down today," Rosemary said, "and I'm quite sure he is, he'd be really happy to see all of you because I know it was his friends from town, from this little town, that he cherished the most. The air force moved him all over the place and finally sent him halfway around the world, but he still said the best place he'd ever been was right here. And if you don't believe me, I think I can show you how much he cared about the people here by telling you a story.

"Years ago, when Michael was in the fourth grade, he had a teacher, Mrs. Mooney, who's here today. I know many of you had her too. He got mostly 'Satisfactory' grades on his report card, except in the category of classroom deportment. That didn't have anything to do with getting along well with others, but more with sitting still and keeping quiet and not throwing things around the room—that sort of thing—which Michael sometimes found difficult.

"So one day in class, Michael had been acting up a bit and the whole class was getting stirred up, and I should tell you that it was the day before Christmas vacation, so it was very hard for the kids to concentrate. I imagine Mrs. Mooney just wanted some peace and quiet, so she came up with an assignment to keep the class occupied. This was about the time the Vietnam War was ending and the OPEC embargo was causing fuel shortages and everyone was watching the television for news about Watergate and there was just a lot of negativity everywhere you looked.

"Mrs. Mooney decided to do something to stress the positive for a change. So she told everyone in the class to take out a piece of paper. She told them they were going to make out a Christmas list, except that instead of listing things they wanted, they were going to give each other gifts in words. She told them to write their names at the top of the page, then pass their papers to the student next to them. What they were supposed to do was write down something they liked about the person whose name was at the top."

James looked to the right to see Mrs. Mooney listening with her eyes closed and nodding rhythmically. He looked across the aisle where Sarah sat with Terry and Martha, a few pews up from where he and his parents were sitting. Sarah leaned over to whisper something to Martha. He wondered what she was saying.

Rosemary continued, "Mrs. Mooney stressed that there was to be no teasing and no kidding around. Everybody had to take the assignment seriously and really think about what they liked about the person at the top of the page. And when they were finished writing, they passed the piece of paper to the person next to them on the right, and so on and so forth, so that when they were done, they'd each have twenty-four nice things to read about themselves."

She paused. She took another sip of water and a deep breath.

"Well, to make a long story short, when Michael died, he had his list with him. All these years later. When Michael came home, the air force sent his effects along, and we went through his wallet and found the list in a small waterproof plastic pouch, the kind you might keep credit cards in. He never talked about it to us, but the fact that he carried it with him is a pretty good indication of how much it meant to him and how much the people he grew up with mattered to him. Let me read a few things to you."

She held up a thin, creased sheet of notebook paper and began to read.

"'I like the way you smile.'

"'I like how you never cut in line.'

"'I like how you let me borrow your mitt sometimes.'

"'When we play baseball and you pitch you let me hit it.'

"'I like it when you make a joke.'

"'I like when you gave me half your sandwich because I forgot mine and you said you weren't hungry but I knew that was not true.'

"'I like it when you say my name instead of hey you.'

"'Thank you for coming to my birthday party.'

"'I like it when you let me ride your bike and when my dad ran over it in the driveway you didn't get mad.'

"'I like it when we play pig-pile and you don't jump on me when I'm it because you're too big.'

"'I like it when some older kids were bothering me you said go away and they did.'

"'You're pretty good with machines and building stuff, though you obviously don't know the first thing about making a tree house.' I'm not sure who wrote that one."

Sarah turned and shot James a look. Rosemary continued reading.

"'I like it because you don't do your homework, so I don't have to either.'

"'I like how you can hit things with a rock.'

"'I liked it when you showed me how to make a paper airplane.'

"'I like your hair.'

"'I like you to laugh with.'

"'I like it when you put stuff in your nose.'

"'I think you're the best friend a person could have.'

"That was my brother," said Rosemary as she refolded the sheet of paper. "And even though we're going to miss him like crazy for a long time, I can't believe how lucky we were to ever have had him. I feel sorry for the people who never knew him, because we are all more fortunate than them. And in that, we can rejoice."

Thirteen

THE PARKING LOT AT THE SUPPER CLUB WAS FULL. James had gone home to get his car, uncertain how long he might want to stay.

Sarah was holding a place at her table for him when he arrived. He thought again how she looked different somehow, chic and elegant, two words James never expected would apply to the tomboy who'd thrown dead fish at him at the quarry. Julie was right—Sarah had changed, one of those women, James allowed, who bloom in their twenties. Her slightly reddened nose made her even more endearing.

"Hi, Sarah," he told her. "You look nice."

She looked slightly shocked.

"What did you say?" she asked.

"I said you look nice."

"That's what I thought you said," she told him, then smiled. "Thank you. You look nice too."

He looked around. There was a buffet set up against the wall, and a country band played from the stage, keeping it mellow so people didn't have to shout to be heard. James remembered how fond Mike had been of country music, long before anybody else in the area thought country was cool, popping cartridges of Johnny Cash and Charlie Rich and Hank Williams into the eight-track player in his car.

When the band stopped, Father Costello, still in his clerical collar but wearing a sport coat over a black shirt, took the microphone and explained that the Quinn family had asked him to open with a brief prayer.

"Our heavenly Father," he said, "we ask you now for your blessing. And we ask that you might look down on those of us gathered here tonight and unite us in Christian love, as well as in remembrance of our departed friend, Michael Quinn. Grant that we might be filled not only with the Holy Spirit but also one more time with the spirit of Mike Quinn, whose uncontainable joy for living filled any room he entered and enlivened those around him. In Jesus' name we pray. Amen."

After Father Costello finished, he smiled at the crowd.

"Now for those of you who may not be familiar with the concept, we Catholics have a tradition of the wake, which was originally a watch kept over the body of the deceased prior to burial. Clearly we're doing things a little differently tonight. In more recent times, I like to think of the wake as a chance to bring the loved one back to life and to give them a place in our hearts by telling stories and talking about them, and that's really all this night is about. We're keeping watch over Michael's memory, and we're bearing witness. That said, I'd like to invite anybody who wants to to come on up here and take the microphone and share your memories with the rest of us. It's very informal, so please don't be afraid."

James and Sarah were sitting at a table with Martha and Terry. Ben Larson joined them after they were already seated, sitting on the other side of Sarah from James. James had looked for Ben Larson after the service but couldn't find him. He wanted to apologize to Ben for being short with him the night before, but there didn't seem to be a good moment to say anything.

The first speaker was a man from Mike's unit who was stateside recuperating from an injury. Captain Thomas Farrell said he'd driven down from St. Paul for the occasion and told the crowd he considered it an honor and a privilege to represent the military today.

"I'll be brief," Captain Farrell said, "because I know there are a lot of other people who want to say something. Basically, I knew two Mike Quinns. The first was the on-duty Captain Michael Quinn, who was as good a flier as any man who ever served, I can say with all truthfulness. He inspired the utmost confidence. The fact that he'd been a mechanic before becoming a pilot meant he knew that machine inside and out, literally. There was nobody in the unit who wouldn't have flown with him.

"The family asked me to explain to you a little bit about the accident. The dust storm that Mike got caught in was both massive and sudden. I don't know how many of you have ever been in a desert like that, but it's remarkable how fast conditions can change, and despite all the safeguards and air filters and what have you, in this case the dust just overwhelmed the system, and visibility was zero. Colonel Cruz told me that even then, with his systems failing, Mike almost managed to set her down. But at the last minute, when the dust cleared a little bit, he saw that he was coming down on top of a village, so he used the last of his power to clear that. So the air force wants his family and you all to know that Michael Quinn was truly a hero and will be decorated as such.

"Anyway, that's the on-duty Mike Quinn that I knew. The other Mike was the off-duty guy, and I gather most of you knew that person the way I did. He liked motorcycles and dance clubs. And he liked to test the beer when we went to taverns in the countries we'd visit on temporary duty—to make sure it was safe for the rest of us to drink. With never a thought for himself. He could be a bit of a wild man, as I'm sure you know. One time in the Philippines we decided we were going to steal the flag of another unit from a flagpole that was sticking out from the second story of a hotel, but they got wind of it and greased the last three feet of the flagpole. Well, Mike went for it anyway and managed to grab the flag before he fell and bounced off an awning and landed in the swimming pool. And of course he told us that was the way he'd planned it all along. He was also the possessor of the worst karaoke singing voice any of us had ever heard—possibly the worst voice in the entire United States Armed Forces—but that never stopped him from singing. As Mike's sister said earlier today, we all felt lucky we knew him, and we're all going to miss him."

Applause erupted from several tables as Captain Ferrell sat down, then several other people got up to speak. A couple of James's classmates talked about Mike's wild side, recalling the night he helped steal the twenty-foot-tall fiberglass cowboy from the tire dealership—it was his idea to use a boat trailer—or the time he and a group of buddies used a mixture of bluegrass seed and fertilizer to emboss their school's name on the football field of a rival high school.

James could have said so many things. He was still considering his options when Terry Kesler rose from the table to approach the mike. He introduced himself to anybody who didn't know him and said it would be a lie if he didn't admit that Mike Quinn had a wild side. "But I'd like, if I could, to talk about a different side of Mike, because he could also be really sensible when he had to be. And that was usually when no one else wanted the job.

"Some of you maybe know how I got a little crazy myself a couple years back," Terry said, "when the bank wanted to take my bin. And I got pretty angry, 'cause I kept up my end of the bargain and I couldn't understand why they didn't keep theirs. Anyways, I lost my equity. And that wasn't anybody's fault—nobody in particular, anyway—unless it was my fault for borrowing so much money in the first place when I shoulda been more careful.

"I don't want to get into that anymore, except to say I got really mad one night, and then I got really drunk, and I decided I was gonna bash my bin in so that if they wanted to repossess it, they could come and get it, you know, but it was gonna be in pieces when they got there. And it was. And I never told anybody, but I guess it doesn't matter now, so I can tell you that Mike was there too that night. He was home on leave. And at first he tried to talk me out of it and told me I was gonna get in trouble. But when I said I was gonna do it anyway because I didn't care, he said, 'Well, in that case I better supervise to make sure you don't dump the whole thing on your head.'

"I got arrested, and really, I pretty much fell apart after that and got into all sorts of stuff. What I'm saying is, it would have been a lot worse except that Mike was there every step of the way with me, trying to get me to clean up my act, and when I couldn't, it was Mike who drove me to the treatment center where I finally got sober. And I have been sober ever since. So I owe it to my higher power, but I also owe it to Mike, really, more'n anything."

He started to leave the stage, then returned to the microphone.

"One other thing I wanted to say," Terry said. "I was thinking about what Mike's sister said this afternoon, about how when they went through Mike's stuff, they found out he had that list on him. And just in case anybody thought that was weird or something, I got mine too."

He reached into his back pocket, pulled out his wallet, and took from it a heavily worn piece of folded paper, which he held up for all to see.

"I ain't ashamed to say so. I just didn't want anybody thinking less of Mike 'cause he had his."

Terry took his seat. James wanted to cry, though he couldn't

immediately identify the reasons why. Why was it so hard for
men to admit they needed other people? Why was it so hard for
him? He felt Sarah's hand on his arm.

"Are you all right?" she whispered. He only nodded. Ben
stared at the stage, looking stony and unmoved, though the way
he blinked his eyes gave him away. When Terry sat back down,
Martha looked at her husband in shock.

"How long have you had that list?"

"Ever since," Terry said. "Ever since we wrote 'em."

"Why didn't you tell me?"

"I'm supposed to tell you everything that's in my wallet?" he
said. "You can read it if you want to. Sometimes when I feel like
I want a drink, I take it out and read it, that's all."

But Martha wasn't angry. Instead, she reached under her
seat, opened her purse, and searched in it until she found what
she was looking for, a small, thin black box resembling a cigarette holder. She opened it and took out a folded piece of paper,
which she placed on the table next to Terry's. He looked at her,
then smiled.

"Aren't you just full of surprises," he told his wife.

"You have yours too?" Sarah asked.

"What?" Martha said defensively. "What's the big deal? You guys—my dad kept telling me I was an unworthy sinner who needed to repent. You were lucky—you only heard it on Sundays. I needed to hear from somebody that I wasn't such a bad person."

Terry and Martha read each other's lists.

"You see?" Terry said, reading. "Somebody thought you were cool." He turned to the rest of the table. "She always thought she was a dork."

"That would be me," Sarah said. "I wrote that."

"You thought I was cool?" Martha said. Sarah nodded. "Why?"

"I don't know," Sarah said. "You were so defiant. I was always trying to be like that, but I always knew I was faking it. You were the real deal."

"Did she ever tell you about the time—" Terry began, but Sarah interrupted him, pointing at the stage, where one of their classmates stood at the microphone, holding a piece of paper over her head.

"We just found out," the classmate said, "that two people at our table had their lists on them, so we wanted to take a survey.

How many people here who were in Mrs. Mooney's class still have their lists?"

In a booth across the room, a classmate held his hand up high, waving a piece of paper. Then another in the booth next to him. Soon there were arms in the air at nearly every table—a total of nineteen people who still carried their Christmas lists with them.

"HOW ABOUT YOU, BEN?" SARAH ASKED. "WHERE'S yours?"

"I have no idea," he said.

"None?"

"None. Didn't save it. Never felt the need, I guess," he said.

"Geez, Benny," Sarah said. "It's okay, you know? You can lower your shields—you're among friends." He indicated by his lack of response that he didn't want to talk about it. Martha and Terry had moved to the stage, where everyone was comparing lists. When Martha motioned to Sarah to join her, Sarah said, "Will you guys excuse me for a second?" Then she leaned over and whispered in James's ear, "Don't go—I want to talk to you."

James was still in a daze. He felt oddly vulnerable, as if some sort of defense mechanism he hadn't known was in place had suddenly begun to crumble. He thought of Catherine's words when they'd met for coffee the night before he drove home for the holidays.

"You keep everybody at arm's length," she'd said. "I'm not saying this to be mean, but sometimes you're your own worst enemy. And the irony is that you're so well defended that the only enemy who could break through the walls you put up is you. It's like you think love is some sort of debt you have to repay. Or like you don't deserve it. Sometimes when I tell you I love you, I almost get the impression you don't want to hear it, even though I know at some level you do. I thought I could overcome that, but I can't. I'm sorry. I tried. So drive safe and have a merry Christmas. I know maybe that's hard to hear right now, but I do mean it. This is for the best. And tell your family . . . I'm sorry."

He looked at Ben, the only other person left at the table now. Sarah had always told him he and Ben were more alike than either one of them wanted to admit.

"What are you staring at?" Ben asked him.

"She's right, you know," James said.

"About what?"

"About the whole stiff-arm thing," he said. "Keeping your friends from getting too close. Did I ever tell you how jealous I was of you?"

"You were jealous of me?"

"Yeah."

"For what?"

"For all the time you had with Sarah. Every summer I came home, I felt like I had to win her back because I was afraid someone was going to steal my friend away."

"Well, for the record," Ben said, "she still likes you better. Man, I feel like we're a couple of girls, passing notes in homeroom. She likes you, all right?"

"What do you mean, she likes me?"

"God, Engler, you were always so dense. She told me. She always liked you, but she was always too embarrassed to tell you. And you were always too stupid to realize what was right in front of you. It's like talking to a chicken."

James briefly wondered how Ben knew what it was like to talk to a chicken. Perhaps it was a new language skill he'd picked up at the commodities exchange.

Ben stood up, leaving James alone at the table.

James felt a thousand things. At one moment he felt like he was looking down on himself from an airplane five miles up, and from that distance it seemed ineffably strange to be in there, in a small snowy town, in a corny old restaurant, surrounded by bad holiday sweaters and iceberg lettuce. The next moment he felt perfectly at home, like he'd never meant to leave. When he thought of Catherine, he thought that love was impossible, but when he thought of all the couples he knew who'd been married all their lives—his own parents, the Larsons, the Gruenings, the Quinns— it seemed perhaps not as difficult as he thought.

So what was the key? The secret? He felt like it was right there in front of him but still just beyond his reach. When he remembered Mike, or Gerry, life seemed too fragile and too tragic to bear, but when he looked out the window at the snow falling in the night, he sensed there was something healing in the cycle of the seasons, death and rebirth, a time to sleep and a time to awaken.

What was it? What was the secret—or was it obvious to everyone else and a mystery only to him? He felt strange, confused, adrift. He needed to know something, and he didn't know what that thing was, but he did know where to look for it.

Sarah caught up to him just as he'd reached his car. She'd left her coat inside.

"Where are you going?" she asked.

"I have to go home," he told her.

"Do you know where your list is?" she asked.

He briefly considered pretending he didn't care, the way Ben had, but he knew Sarah wasn't going to buy it.

"My mother saved everything," he said. "If I still have it, it'll be in the attic. How about you—where's yours?"

"Mine's at my house, locked up in my diary."

"The pink one with the picture of David Cassidy glued inside the cover?"

"You read my diary?"

"You let me," he said. "You made me promise never to tell anybody."

"You're gonna get through this, you know," she said. "You will get over her. You didn't do anything wrong. It's not like you ran a school bus off a mountain road."

"I know," he said. He wanted to tell her how grateful he was, how much her friendship meant to him. He wanted to tell her a thousand things, but first he wanted to go home.

"Will I see you before you leave town?" she said.

"I'll call you."

She looked at him.

"You always say that, you know," she said. "Every time you left, you used to say you'd call me, and then you wouldn't. And I always forgave you. But this time I won't."

"I'll call you," he said. "I will."

At first his car wouldn't start, and for a while he thought he'd have to walk. Then the ignition caught on the third try and the engine roared to life. He saw Sarah standing in his headlights without a coat on, her arms folded across her chest for warmth. She made the sign of a telephone, extending the thumb and little finger of her right hand, and waggled it at him emphatically, then waved good-bye.

HE DROVE SLOWLY BECAUSE IT WAS SNOWING AGAIN, though nothing like the blizzard two days ago. The world seemed impossibly quiet, with only the sound of his wheels crunching the snow. His hometown had never seemed so beautiful, he thought, or so peaceful. He drove past houses where, through the parted curtains, he saw Christmas trees lit. He passed one house where the residents had already left their tree on the curb for the trucks to pick up. That seemed a bit impatient.

When he reached First Emmanuel, he had to stop to wait for the light to change. He looked at the crèche. He could still hear his father reading the passage from Luke, the story of Jesus' birth. The figurines in the crèche were large and made of solid concrete to prevent vandals from carrying them off, except for baby Jesus in the manger, which was portrayed by a more lifelike plastic baby doll. He thought of his father's words. "You never stop loving your children—you can't." He tried to imagine how much love you'd have to have to give the world your only son. It was truly beyond imagining, and wasn't that where faith began— where imagination left off? He was a day late, but he felt like now he finally heard what he wasn't listening for on Christmas Eve.

He kept driving.

The road to the house ran alongside the country club's six-teenth fairway, where he saw two boys sledding in the darkness, wearing headlamps to light their way. This one was a much gen-tler slope than Dead Man's Hill, but still a challenge. He remem-bered the boundless enthusiasm he'd once had, before he started brooding and ruminating on everything. He remembered living in the moment without fear of consequence, throwing himself at life with a child's unquenchable zest. Where had it gone? Was it gone forever? Mike had hung on to his sense of wonder. Perhaps, James thought, his own was recoverable.

When he got home, he hurried to the attic, where his mother had archived everyone's things. It was cold in the uninsulated room, with windows left open at either end to let the house breathe, so he kept on his coat as he rummaged through the boxes and file cabinets. His mother had had plenty of office materials to work with—antiquated file cabinets and manila envelopes and folders James's father brought home from the bank. James was thankful for her organizational skills because he easily found what he was looking for: a box labeled "James: 1970–1975" in magic marker and a folder marked "Grade 4/1972."

His list had been folded once and slipped into a protective plastic sheath. He'd written his name, James B. Engler, in capital letters half an inch high, centered at the top. He read his Christmas list by the light of a bare, sixty-watt light bulb, his breath steaming in the cold air.

"I think you're a good writer," his list began.

"I like your dad's car." He couldn't really take credit for that one, but it was still better than someone saying they hated his dad's car.

"I like my sides hurt when you make me laugh," the next person said. He'd always remembered jokes.

"I like how you do everything I tell you to because I am the all-knowing Master of the Univers and you are simple a robot I built to surve me and don't even know it. You think your real, your pathetic, and you don't know how to build a treehouse either but I like you anyway and if I had to fall out of a tree with somebody its you."

He smiled. That was, he could recall with certainty, Mike's contribution. And that, James realized, was how you had to love—risking everything, holding nothing back, no matter how much it might hurt to fall out of a tree, or out of love, or from grace. You didn't hold back from loving for fear that you might lose what you love. You loved precisely because you could— indeed, would—one day lose what you love. You'd lose everything in the end. It was what you did with your life in the meantime that mattered, how you carried forward your part of the conversation.

When Gerry died, the part that had hurt the most was being unable to talk to him again. James had been eating his words ever since.

And now he was remembering something else. The last thing his brother said hadn't been, "Don't sweat it, Squirt." What he'd said was, "Don't sweat it, Squirt. I love you even if you are a twerp sometimes." James had never gotten the chance to say "I love you" back.

"I like your stories."

"I think you're smart."

"I like the way you make up things."

"I like the way you don't usually lie because you're honest." Catherine had told him she didn't think he was entirely honest with himself. If he was entirely honest with himself, he had to admit she was right. He was afraid of love, he realized, because he didn't feel worthy of it. He hadn't felt worthy in a long time— not since Gerry died, at least. So he held back. He shouldn't.

"I like how you know things and places."

"I like you can spell good."

"I like how you remember things." What things were those? he tried to recall.

"I like it when you make a joke."

"I don't know why I like you, but I do."

"I like your smile."

"I like your smile too." He wondered if that was Terry, who frequently copied from the person sitting next to him.

"You give good book reports and you read a lot."

"I think you are very sincere." He wondered who'd known what the word *sincere* meant.

"I like when you read you move your lips—did you know that?"

"I think you have great handwriting."

"You are not as stupid as some people." He couldn't be sure, but that sounded like the kind of thing Ben Larson would have written.

The list made him want to cry.

He remembered what he'd done with it when he got home from school, how he couldn't accept the things that were written there because no one knew how ashamed he felt, and how he'd left his list on the kitchen table for his mother to find, hoping she'd show it to his father, hoping he'd say something to him, hoping he'd say something to take the shame away—though of course, James himself was the only one who could do that. The kid the list described had a pretty good chance of growing into a decent human being. The list described someone with an essential core of goodness, and that remained intact, even if it was a bit buried beneath the baggage of adulthood.

He pulled the string to turn off the light. He felt almost light-headed, calm and happy for the first time in months. He was heading downstairs when he heard the phone ringing.

Fourteen

"I TOLD YOU I WAS GOING TO CALL YOU," HE SAID.

"Well, I wasn't taking any chances," Sarah said. "Did you find it?"

"I found it," he said.

"So what'd it say?"

"A lot of things," he said. "Mostly that I was a good writer. Other things. How about you?"

"I found mine," she said. "You signed yours."

"I signed my what?"

"The thing you wrote on my list. You signed it. You are such a doofus."

"Why?" he asked. "What'd I write?"

"By the way, everybody else said I was brilliant and smart and funny. Just so you know."

"You're all those things," he said. "What'd I write?"

"Can I read it to you?" she asked. She read, "'I like everything about you. I can't pick one thing, but I think you should know you're a lot prettier than you think you are. I think you could be the prettiest girl in the whole class if you wanted to be.' That's what you wrote. And you were the only one who said anything like that."

"Well, I meant it," he said.

"Did you really think that?"

"I really thought that," he told her. "Really."

"Well then, thank you," she said. "Because I sure didn't think so. Not to sound superficial, but I thought I was the Little Mouse on the Prairie. I thought every other girl had better hair than me, or better . . . anyway, I didn't think I was much of a girl. On the playground, I had all the confidence in the world, but as a girl, I never . . . I thought I was ugly."

"You thought you were ugly?" he said. "That's ridiculous."

"I just really needed to hear what it was you said," she told him. "So thank you. And thank you for not teasing me."

"You know why I used to do that, don't you? Why I teased you?"

"Why?"

"Because I liked you so·much but was too afraid to tell you. I was at the stage where if a boy likes a girl, he'll hit her or throw disgusting things at her. I think chimpanzees do the same thing."

"You must have really liked me, then," she said, "because you threw a lot of disgusting things at me."

"As I recall, you threw a dead fish at me."

"One dead fish," she said. "That doesn't mean—"

"What?"

"Nothing," she said. "So what stage are you at now?"

"In transition," he said. "I've decided I need to be more emotionally honest. Did you know, for instance, that I've loved you my whole life? It's like what you said on my list. I think it's funny that we both signed what we wrote."

There was silence on the other end of the phone.

"Hello?" he said.

"I'm still here. Why?" she asked. "What'd I say?"

"You don't remember?"

"I don't remember. Whatever it was—"

He heard his phone beep.

"Can you hang on a second?" he asked her. "I've got another call coming."

"Well, all right," she said, "but don't keep me waiting."

"One sec, I promise," he said, hitting the flash button.

BEN LARSON WAS ON THE OTHER LINE.

"Hey, Ben," James said. "What's up? Everything okay?" He heard familiar singing in the background.

"Everything's good," Ben said. "As you can probably tell, the Merry Madrigals are downstairs wassailing and singing *Jingle Bell Rock*, but other than that, all is calm and bright."

He'd wondered why his parents weren't there when he'd returned home.

"That's good to hear," he said, waiting.

"I won't keep you," Ben said, "but I wanted to tell you something. You're right. And I lied. Okay? I knew exactly where my list was, and I just reread it. I do keep people at a distance. That wasn't the first time I've been told that. I'm working on it. You told me on my list. You wrote, 'All you need is love.' And you signed it."

"I signed everybody's," James said. "I was quoting the Beatles."

"You were?" Ben said. "Oh, right. Of course you were. I never thought of that. I thought you were talking to me directly."

"Well, I was," James said, "but, you know, it's kind of weird if you say stuff like that to your friends. It's a lot easier if you can quote from a song."

"Got it," Ben said. "Anyway, you were right. And I was out of line at church when I said what I said about your folks. I didn't realize there'd been a screw-up. My folks were really hurt when yours didn't come. I didn't know they never got the invitation."

"Not a problem," James said. "We thought they hadn't been invited. I'm sorry too. I overreacted."

"Well," Ben said. "I don't want to keep you. I just wanted to call to say that."

"Okay," James said. "Merry Christmas, Ben."

"Merry Christmas, Jim," Ben said.

"And thanks for the heads up, too," James said. "About Sarah."

"You owe me," Ben said.

"I do," James said.

HE PRESSED THE FLASH BUTTON AGAIN.

"The suspense is killing me," Sarah said. "Who was that?"

"That was Ben. He wanted me to know he lied about throwing away his list. He had it all along."

"See?" she said. "I told you."

She paused.

"What?" he asked. "What is it?"

"It's stupid," she told him. "Honestly? I was terrified that that was Catherine calling, saying she wanted you back or something. And that you were going to tell me how excited you were about seeing her again when you get back to New York. Something like that . . . J.B., are you still there?"

"Forward," he said.

"Pardon me?"

"You asked me if I had a time machine, would I go forward or backward, and I said I didn't know the answer. Now I do. Forward. Full speed ahead."

"That's good," Sarah said. "That's kind of a breakthrough then."

"It is," he agreed.

"So what did I say on your list?" she said. "I want to know."

"It's pretty embarrassing, really," he said.

"What is it?"

"I really think I need to show you in person," he said. "What are you doing for breakfast?"

"Tell me now."

"I have to show you," he said. "Otherwise you'll think I'm making it up. How about the Country Kitchen, tomorrow morning at eight?"

Fifteen

HE KNEW HE COULDN'T GO TO BED UNTIL HE MADE one more call, but it was ten-thirty and he wasn't sure if the person he needed to call was still awake, so he got back in his car and drove to the address he'd found in the telephone book. Mrs. Mooney lived in a white Cape Cod–style, one-and-a-half-story home at the edge of town, near the cemetery. Her windows were all lit and he saw a silhouette moving beyond the curtains, so apparently it wasn't too late. He considered going home and using the phone, but he was here, and he wanted to tell her something.

The driveway and the walk had been cleared of snow by somebody with a snowblower. He saw where she'd placed inverted V-shaped stiles over her bushes to protected them from the snow. A cheery wreath hung from the doorknocker, which he used, giving it a shave-and-a-haircut cadence lest she think a knock on the door this late at night signaled trouble. The door opened only the length of its six-inch security chain before she saw who it was and opened it completely. James was surprised to see her wearing a jogging suit and tennis shoes. He looked at the television. Some sort of exercise video was paused on the VCR.

She looked puzzled.

"Hello, James," she said. "Is everything all right?"

"Everything is good," he said. "I don't want to worry you, and I know it's terribly late to be stopping by, but I saw your lights on, and I wasn't sure how early in the morning you'd be leaving."

"Come in, come in," she said. "Don't worry about the hour. I've been a night owl all my life. Come in and take your coat off. Can I get you some coffee or a can of pop?"

"No, no," he said, "thank you. I'm not staying, but I needed to talk to you very briefly—I won't keep you." He saw a pair of suitcases packed and waiting by the door in the kitchen that led to the garage. The whole house smelled of some sort of apple and spice potpourri.

"You're sure you're all right?" she asked.

"Yes, I'm quite all right," he said. "Did anybody call you tonight? After the party?"

She shook her head.

"I don't think so," she said. "I was talking to my sister in San Diego for quite a while."

"Then I have to tell you something," he told her. "I think you're going to want to hear this." He related, as exactly as he could, what had happened that night—how the group had discovered that so many of them had carried their Christmas lists with them. She nodded as she listened, looking him in the eye and occasionally widening her eyes in surprise. When he'd finished, she put her hand over her heart and said, "Well, isn't that something? How many had their lists with them, did you say?"

"Nineteen," he said. "And I went home and found mine in the attic."

"Really," she said. She smiled. "Well, what do you know? I don't believe I ever would have thought. . . ."

"I wanted to call you to tell you, but I was afraid you'd have gone to bed," he said, "so I drove over just to see if you were still up, and then I figured, as long as I was here, I'd tell you in person."

"I'm glad you did, James," she said. "I'm quite glad that you did."

"I just thought," he said, "that the whole point was to tell people how much you cared about them and how much they meant to you, but then I thought how we probably never told you how much you meant to us. And you should know."

"Oh, you all told me in many other ways," she said dismissively, as if the idea embarrassed her. "But thank you. I do indeed appreciate your stopping by. You know, I don't want to say anything critical of where you live, but I just can't imagine how it would be to teach in a large city, where you never get the opportunity to see your students grow up. In this little town, with all the people I run into, I get the chance nearly every day to see that I just may have done some good. I suppose other people have to take it on faith. But thank you for telling me."

"I'm going to take that teaching job I told you about," James told her. "And it's in a small town, by the way. So any advice before I go?"

"Well," she said, smiling, "just make sure your students know they're special. Each one of them. I know that sounds like the world's oldest cliché, but you know, I think more and more in this day and age of all these rock-and-roll stars and celebrities everywhere—" She paused. "Young people think they have to be on television before they're important. I'm afraid that too many of them are going to grow up disappointed. That's all I ever did, really—try to make you all realize how unique you were."

"Well, you're pretty unique too, I think," he said, rising to leave.

"Merry Christmas, James Engler," Mrs. Mooney said. "And give that girlfriend of yours a hug from me too."

He supposed she was referring to Sarah. He felt no need to clear up the misconception.

"I will," he said.

Epilogue

PATRICK LOOKED AT ME.

"So what happened next?" he asked with a bit of a smirk on his face, playing along with the conceit that the characters in the story I'd told him were fictitious. "Did they meet for breakfast?"

"They did indeed," I told him.

"Did he kiss her?" Patrick asked. "Tell me he kissed her."

Sarah was in the other room, answering a phone call that apparently wasn't for me. It had rung several hours earlier, and I feared some other *crisis was impinging on our already eventful evening, but I trusted Sarah to handle it.*

"Well, they had a very interesting conversation," I said. "They were both cautious about rushing into anything, which they thought was pretty funny since they'd known each other since they were four. Anyway, they made plans for her to come out to visit him in New York, and they took it slow since they were getting to know each other in an entirely different way."

"Did he kiss her?"

"Why are you so interested in that?"

"Just tell me he kissed her."

"He kissed her," I said. "It was quite a memorable kiss."

"So, what'd she write? On his list?"

"First things first," I said. "Don't you want to know what happened to everybody else?"

Very briefly, I wrapped up the story.

THE GULF WAR COMMENCED ON JANUARY 17, AND A cease-fire was declared on March 2. In Onagle, things calmed down at the bank as the industry recovered during the Clinton years. Walter Engler turned the bank over to Joe, who moved

Lisa and the girls into the house after Walter and Ruth retired to Tucson. Lisa and Joe tried one more time to get pregnant and had a third child, a boy they named Gerald Walter. Joe finally quit smoking the day his son was born and sang him lullabies every night. Lisa built a greenhouse on the south side of the house and substantially altered the landscaping. She got the girls involved in 4-H. They adjusted to small-town life, though it took time. They loved their baby brother.

Eric and Rachel and the boys thrived in Colorado but always made it home for Christmas. Thomas's high-school soccer team won the state championship. Henry turned out to be quite an artist. Eric kept the toupee but had it grayed from year to year to match his natural hair.

Julie eventually married a man eight years her senior, a Chicago investment banker named Charles, who was also an accomplished amateur jazz musician. From that point on, at Christmas gatherings Charlie was the one who played the piano, adding flourishes at the end of traditional carols and hymns that made Ruth smile. Julie contracted with a gallery in New York and another in San Francisco that were delighted to show her work.

James's parents came home for the holidays and for visits but otherwise lived quite happily in Arizona, where his father golfed and his mother gardened, until his father died in his sleep in 1998. When Joe and Lisa invited Ruth to move back in with them, she was reluctant and said she didn't want to be the fifth wheel. When Cully married a woman from Des Moines whom he'd met on the Internet, Ruth finally agreed to move into the cottage, which Cully painted inside and out before he left, but she spent a part of each winter in the house in Arizona to escape the cold. She often entertained visitors from Onagle there, including the Larsons and the Gruenings, who were similarly inclined towards warm winter getaways.

James left Onagle the afternoon following the memorial service and party because he had things in New York to attend to. He spoke to Catherine on the phone, briefly, before New Year's Eve but didn't inquire as to her plans, nor did she inquire as to his. They parted ways amicably but didn't really remain friends, though years later he got a letter from her saying she'd moved to Paris.

After his breakfast with Sarah, he stopped at the cemetery, where he visited two graves, one of "Capt. Michael C. Quinn,

U.S.A.F. 1962–1990" and the other of "Capt. Walter Gerald Engler, U.S.A.F. 1947–1972 Beloved," the latter marked with a slab of white marble with an American flag carved into the face, the former with a temporary cross, placed there until the permanent stone could be delivered.

Someone had left a beer on Mike's grave, and the relatively fresh footprints in the snow indicated that whoever left it had visited the night before. When James found his brother's grave, he took his gloves off and touched the cold stone with his fingers, feeling the words carved there. When he was done, he stood and turned his collar up against the cold.

"I love you too," he said.

He couldn't think of anything he needed to add to that.

Before leaving the cemetery, he sat in his car awhile. He realized that while he still missed his brother and his friend Mike, his sense of loss was supplemented with a larger feeling of gratitude. He felt proud of both men and thankful that he'd had them in his life. It seemed like the right way to look at things.

He had one final errand. He stopped at the shopping center, which was crowded with shoppers looking for post-Christmas bargains, and purchased the best teakettle he could find, an enameled blue beauty that whistled like a train when the water boiled. He had the teakettle gift-wrapped and left it, with a card, on Cully's porch.

As he drove back to New York, James had a long time to think. He thought of his family and his friends and of the dreams he'd once had and of the new dreams he needed to replace them with. He thought as well of his Christmas list. As he did, he found himself revisiting a time when he knew himself as purely good, existing in a state of what had seemed like holy grace. His list had restored the better part of himself—had somehow reminded him how to love.

There had been a time when he had loved every part of his life and everybody in it, every moment of every day, fearlessly and without pause. A time when he couldn't wait to wake up and couldn't wait to go to sleep, when he ran everywhere he went because he wanted to know what was around every corner and behind every closed door and under every closed lid and in every drawer and pocket. A time when every day felt like Christmas morning. That's what he missed. That's what he was now rediscovering.

He did not miss his innocence or regret losing it—that was

natural. What he'd lost sight of didn't really have anything to do with innocence. It was more a matter of knowing his place in the world, of being certain of his membership in the human race and in the sure promise of love, which could appear in the most unexpected places at the most surprising of times, in what could just possibly be a benevolent and loving universe.

"I DON'T KNOW HOW ELSE TO PUT IT," I TOLD *Patrick. "You know how they always say Christmas is about giving, not receiving? Well I'm sorry to be so corny, but it's not just Christmas. Love is about giving. It's about looking out, not looking in, and about loving, not being loved. It's kind of a cliché, I know, but it's really just a question of learning how to be authentic in the way you love, like the way people sing in the shower when they know nobody is listening. You have to live your life the same way, if that makes any sense. And you have to live it forward, like no one's ever broken your heart before or ever will again. Not that you don't learn from the past, but you can't get stuck there. That's what faith is."*

"I think I get it," Patrick said. "So obviously this James character got unstuck as a writer, right?" He looked at me meaningfully. "You said he was having a hard time."

"He did indeed, as soon as he stopped writing fake imitation stories about New Yorkers set in New York, which he didn't know all that much about, and started writing stories about displaced Midwesterners and people and things he did know a little bit about. Of course, some of those stories weren't any good either, but at least the floodgates opened up again. And maybe he never turned into the kind of writer he thought he could be, but he did become the kind of man he wanted to be. It's still a work in progress, needless to say."

Patrick stared at the fire for a while, then looked at me.

"That's the assignment you gave us, wasn't it? The list we made—that's where you got it from, right?"

"That's right," I told him. "I wasn't sure if you remembered."

"I remember," he said. He looked sad again. "But I don't remember what it said. Or where it is. I remember doing it in class. . . ."

"You were in a hurry," I told him. "Your driver was waiting outside, and you had to hurry because you were afraid you were going to miss your flight. You remember that?"

"Yeah," he said.

"I let you go before everybody was finished," I told him.

"I must have left it behind," he said.

"You did," I said.

He looked despondent.

"*Would you like to see it?*" *I asked him.*

"*You saved it?*" *he said.*

"*I save everything,*" *I told him.* "*I am my mother's son. And by the way, I haven't read it.*"

Sarah handed Patrick his list, which she'd retrieved from my files. While Patrick read, my wife asked me to step into the kitchen.

"*What's up?*" *I asked her.* "*Who called? I heard the phone ring, but I assumed you'd tell me if it was important. Is everything all right?*"

"*What's up,*" *she whispered,* "*is we're going to have a visitor. Ellen called from her cell phone. She called earlier too. Asking for directions. And if I'm not mistaken—*" *She looked out the window toward the street. I looked out and saw, much to my surprise, a New York City cab pull into the driveway.* "*Why don't you go tell him someone wants to talk to him?*"

Patrick was reading his list by the fire so intensely that I hadn't had a chance to say anything to him by the time Sarah returned with Patrick's fiancée at her side.

"*Hi, Patrick,*" *Ellen said.*

He turned.

"*First of all,*" *she said apologetically,* "*I need six hundred dollars for the cab.*"

We told them we'd take care of the cab driver and they could pay us back, then closed the door to give them some privacy. The cab driver's name was Najib, and though he politely denied it, it was clear he was starving, so we sat him down in the kitchen and gave him a bowl of stew that Sarah reheated in the microwave. It would have been crazy to try to drive back to the city, so we offered to put him up for the night. When he refused, I made a call and found him a bed and breakfast that had a vacancy and let him use our phone to call his family.

Patrick and Ellen were still talking by the time Sarah and I went to bed. Before she joined me, Sarah threw an extra pillow on the hide-a-bed and left the light on in the study.

Patrick helped me shovel out the driveway the next morning. Our departure time was set for five, but the storm had stopped, and the eight-hundred number I called said our flight to the Twin Cities was still on schedule. Paul and Thomas would be driving up from Onagle to meet us. Our daughter, Amanda, had been on the phone all morning long-distance with her cousin Abigail, planning some sort of surprise during the Christmas Eve program. Our sons, Michael and Simon, returned from their sleepover, barely said hello, changed, and were off to morning hockey practice. Sarah asked them to take care not to get a black eye or a chipped tooth because my mother had said she wanted to get a family photograph taken with all the cousins.

When we were finished shoveling, Patrick and I joined Ellen and

Sarah in the kitchen, and then the four of us had breakfast, featuring waffles swimming in Mill River Academy Grade A Golden Amber Syrup.

"I called the garage," Sarah told Patrick, passing him the bacon. "They said your car is ready. Jim can give you a ride to go pick it up. They said they were pulling cars out of the snow all night."

"You've done enough," Ellen said. "We'll take a cab to the garage."

"Nonsense," Sarah said. "Plus, unless you can get hold of your friend Najib, I doubt you'll be able to find a cab in this town on a Saturday morning. Did you sleep all right?"

"Fine, thank you," Patrick said, stifling a yawn. "Could have used more of it, but what we got was good."

"So what are your plans?" I asked him.

"Immediate or long-term?" he asked. "Immediate is, we're going down to D.C. to see my dad. Long-term, we're going back to Iowa, and I'm going to give the program another try."

"I think that's a good decision," I told him.

"I think the reason I feel so blocked," Patrick said, "has more to do with my father than with the work itself or the things people say in workshops. I'm afraid of letting him down. But I'm not going to worry about that anymore. Did I tell you I realized I've never written a story about family? I've never written about a father-and-son relationship. I've never written about two parents who get divorced. I've been avoiding all of that because I've been afraid of hurting anybody's feelings. I'm going to stop doing that. They say you're supposed to write what you know, don't they?"

"They do say that," I told him. "But you can make stuff up too."

"It sounds like you're asking the right questions," Sarah said. "How about you, Ellen? What are your plans? You're getting your M.F.A. in— what was it?"

"Painting," she said, turning to me. "By the way, Patrick tells me Jules Engler is your sister? I didn't know that."

"That was one of her paintings in the study," I said.

"I know. I was looking at it. She's terrific," Ellen said.

"So you'll go back to finish your degree?" Sarah asked. Ellen nodded as she sipped her coffee. Sarah looked from Ellen to Patrick and back again.

"Oh, and the engagement is back on, by the way," Ellen said.

"It was never really off," Patrick countered.

"We'll talk about that at a later date," Ellen told him, cutting him off with a smile. "The elope thing has changed. I just have to figure a way to stop my parents from spending a fortune on a big wedding they can't afford. I have four married brothers, so I'm sure my parents think they owe it to somebody."

"Can we send you an invitation?" Patrick said, looking at me. "We were *talking about it . . . and we were thinking that if we do something formal, we'd like you to be one of the readers."*

"I'd be flattered," I said. He looked at me. "What?"

"You never did tell me what Sarah wrote on your list," Patrick said.

"No," I said, "and I'm not going to, I'm afraid. I've been sworn to secrecy."

"Oh, come on," Ellen said. "You have to tell us."

"Can't do it," I said. "I said I'd never tell. And there's no part of 'never' that I don't understand."

Sarah smiled.

We drove them to pick up their car. The sun was out, and it was blinding, reflecting off the newly fallen snow, the sky an unbelievable blue. The weather report said seventeen inches had fallen, but the plows had been out all morning and the roads were mostly clear. Sarah had to run to the fabric store to pick up something she needed to finish off the fleece coat she'd made for her mother. She'd packed twice as many clothes as we were going to need, but that was her, always carrying too much stuff. I still had a few loose ends to tie up at my office, but I said I could walk there from the garage. I gave her the cell phone and checked the tires on the car to make sure they were properly inflated, then watched her lead Patrick and Ellen to the highway. I felt the pang I always felt, the fear that something terrible could happen and

I'd never see her again, but the feeling passed when I remembered how lucky I was.

Before he left, Patrick took me aside and asked, "Do you mind if I say something that might be none of my business?" When I told him I didn't mind, he said, "You really should write up the story you told me. It's a good one."

I said I'd think about it.

The walk to my office was brisk and invigorating. All sorts of people were out shoveling their walks and driveways. I walked in the street, where three people passed me in the opposite direction on cross-country skis. An old man driving a red-and-white 1953 Mercury station wagon, a Christmas tree tied to the roof, even stopped and asked me if I needed a lift.

Before I started working, I opened the drawer where I keep my Christmas list and read it again. My eyes were drawn to the last item on my list—last because Sarah had been sitting right next to me in class—the words written in a girlish script with little circles over the letter i that still embarrass my wife, who has since given me permission to reveal what it was she wrote. If she hadn't, I would not include it here.

"You, J.B., are a great guy," she wrote, "and some day, I'm going to marry you. Love, Sarah."

There may have been a series of X's and O's after that, and perhaps a smiley face or two, but if so, I choose not to mention them for fear of embarrassing her further. My list and what she wrote on it changed my life forever, at a time when I was in serious trouble.

Most Christmas lists name the gifts we want. Mine contained the only thing I really need, which is love. More to the point, it taught me how to give love in a word of kindness or praise, or in whatever words the heart chooses to speak, to tell the people we love that we love them, and how we love them, and why we love them, as often as they need to hear it, or when they don't know they need it—or just "because," expecting nothing in return. We risk everything when we do that, but that's the way it should be every time—holding nothing back, staying permanently open to all possibilities, because the love you give away comes back to you, multiplied and magnified, for as long as your heart can beat.

All right, I was wrong. I said earlier that if my story were to address the key to happiness or the "true meaning of Christmas," it would be coincidental, and that I couldn't say what either of those two things might be for anybody but myself. Yet if learning how to give and receive love is not universally important, then I guess I don't know what is. We all approach love differently, but no matter what we say, we all need love, both at Christmas and every other day of the year.